The Spiral Clouds

Musafir Zaman

ISBN: 978-1-958882-11-5

Library of Congress Control Number: 2023933916

Any references to historical events, real people, or real places are used in a fictional context. All other names, characters, and places are products of the author's imagination.

Printed by Farthest Lote Tree Publications, in the United States of America.

First printing edition 2023.

The Farthest Lote Tree Foundation
Del Mar, California

www.farthestlotetree.com

In the Name of God,
the Most Gracious, the Most Merciful

Table of Contents

Climbing to the Light

Climbing
to the Light

From You, 2000 Years Ago

The horse's white mane shone against the setting sun. The sun's petals extended over the sky from a soft candle orange sliding into a sleepy purple. He descended from his horse where his sister awaited him.

The desert sands grew still and solemn. The man, who was more than a man, smiled sadly at her, and at the future which would engulf the world. He saw through blessed sight, and memories of what came and would come flooded through him.

"I will tell your story," she declared, " There will always be those who need to hear it."

They embraced, knowing tomorrow the whole world would change.

***

Projected onto the clouds, a news bulletin crackled over the thunder with its booming announcement: "Narde-ban authorities have discovered the Insurgents." A storm brewed as hovercrafts bolted past the treeless forests and floating streets. When the clouds heaved and when the rain came down to the earth's crusts, the homeless scurried like cockroaches, frantically searching for the smallest divots to disappear into wispy memory. Above the flooding roads, a woman and her husband glanced down.

"Those poor things. I can't bear to see them out there," the wife said with inflated gloom.

"Leader Bliss should really do something about it," the husband said.

"I know! Midan could install a barrier between us and
Level 5. That way we won't have to look at them anymore,"
the wife said, but she didn't really mean it. Watching them
all the way down there gave her a satisfaction she couldn't
describe. She reveled in her sorrow. They turned away and
listened to the rain's slowing thump.

The two seated themselves in front of a holographic monitor
displaying a news anchor, wrapped in a flowing suit tight in
chains of silk and polyester. The anchor reviewed the rise of
the Insurgency. No one knew where and when it began, he
spoke ominously, but its message swept across the country.
To many of the abyss walkers, it seemed like this movement
was like any other. A rare warm breath on a cold night. A
weak, coughing ember to be inevitably swallowed by the
blizzard of Nardeban.

***

Nardeban was not divided by north and south or west
and east but by up and down, a suffocating verticality that
acted as a bridge between the heavens and the earth. Each
city encompassed the corpses of former countries, stitched
together by a series of cities to form mega metropolises rav-
enously licking up any tract of land. Divided into a vertical
order of five levels, the burden of linearity weighed down
on the lowest, trapped furthest in the past, while the levels
bursting free from the clouds held the future in their palms.
The masses took their place below, limited by human ills of
hunger and thirst and want. They sought escape through
drink and drugs, losing themselves with the vain hope of
finding themselves. Walls of pollution, from mistakes long
irreversible, cut the abyss walkers off from the stars. What
bound them together was desolation.

Those few who break free from the chains of gravity rise

past these concerns, floating away to the top. There they forgot the pain at the bottom. But those whose every step lifted above the clouds too sought escape, no different from those below. The further they flew up, the more their minds grew enchanted by the stars, believing they, too, belonged in the sky. But they were invaders of the sky, not its guests. So they may rise, but it makes no difference to the one whose eyes are buried. The ones on the bottom and the ones on the top shared the same thin paper of destiny.

Those who rose above the rest, the highest, those who harnessed the very fusion of the stars to achieve unimagined wonder, these mighty few stood at the head of Nardeban. Secured in these divisions, the mighty who wove the wheels of despair saw the Insurgency as nothing but a stone in the road, one to fall underneath its weight and splinter. The wheel that moves only in revolutions, arrives to crush another.

***

It was over in moments. A spirit sprouting from a single wavering finger to a hundred raised fists over the course of years was slain in a day. Nardeban's army descended from the levels above, bringing its forces to the ground of Level 5, the bottom of the city, the bottom of the world. Tires rumbled over the dirt and smoke spewed from the vehicle's rusted lungs as an army gathered outside the Insurgent threshold. Tanks rolled over the budding stems, returning the land to its barren state. Police officers were indistinguishable from soldiers, all stacked atop one another into a pyramidal command structure, receiving orders and solace as they abandoned responsibility for the wavering finger that pulled the trigger on their enemy. The Insurgents inside the compound fared no better. Their walls of words and rhetoric, like bricks without mortar, collapsed against fear. Within the safety of darkness, they once stood proudly against the system that robbed them of their dignity and their material comfort, but now it robbed them of their will as many fell to their knees. Many, but not all.

The Insurgents rushed out with their arms above their heads. Others remained inside and refused to hand themselves over, knowing of what was to come.

"Forgetfulness is the fountain of sin", one of the committed Insurgents reminded. Another beseeched the deserters to stay, "Choose to leave now and you'll be bathing in it."

"Sure they can attack us, but no bullet can ever graze destiny."

Those outside stood like lambs awaiting slaughter. Once the flag of surrender was raised, the Nardeban commanders gave their signal to attack. Bullets ripped through the air, burrowing in flesh with only screams offered as return fire. Bodies flooded the ground like raindrops. This was not the first time the earth tasted of blood; its heart ached with the memory of time past.

One soldier smiled, proud of his role in reestablishing peace. Maybe things could be better, but violence, he reasoned while reloading his gun, was unacceptable. The world was binary, he thought. Right and wrong, violence and peace, up and down, like the cities of Nardeban themselves. He glanced up, imagining the titanic weight of the four levels above him. Did the lower levelers of Level 5 live with this weight everyday?

Up and down. Verticality. What mattered was how one defined those things, or, more often, how they fell into place on their own. Once, he sympathized with the Insurgents' cause, until he understood what was at stake as they grew. According to Nardeban's news networks, the Insurgency wanted total revolt, determined to sacrifice the bodies of its members in order to build a staircase to reach the top of the levels. They wanted to institute equality, to balance the scales and crush the five levels into one. He closed his eyes and conjured the vision of a giant hand smashing the city at its head, crumbling its soaring spires, covering its coveted stars. The Insurgency's rise was unprecedented but not unpredictable, and his sympathy evolved into apathy and, finally, fear. As an upper leveler, the fears spouted by his holo screens were echoed in his own heart. His life, his family, his possessions. His height, his reach, his stars. The Insurgency claimed to inspire hearts; Nardeban knew how to buy souls. He listened to the higher-ups that prophesied doom and warned him that the Insurgents' messages were lies. The Insurgents wanted neither justice nor equality, and their refusal to approve of Nardeban and demonstrate any gratitude only made them reek of anarchy and chaos. Ideals spewed from their tongues but war tickled at their fingers. In response, Nardeban decided to raid all the Insurgent compounds simultaneously as a show of strength and dominance like a foot stomping down, crushing the hand that dared to reach for the sky.

But there was something else about the Insurgents, something that bugged him as he watched the doors of the Insurgency base. He knew that not all of the Insurgents surrendered. There was no point in resisting, any sensible rebel would cut their losses and pledge their loyalty. Biding their time for another day. It was strategic. At the very least, it spoke of some urge for self-preservation. The people in front of him who were broken into obedience, them he could understand. They fought for themselves, for a better home, for more food on the table. And when they knew they couldn't get it, they cut their losses. This, he understood. Then, why did some remain inside? His rationality strained and faltered. He knew not what they fought for, and his finger itched against the trigger beneath the crescent moon.

The barrage ended as lightning struck, its heavenly flash illuminating the carnage below as all movement came to a halt. One squadron marched forward to enter the building in order to eliminate any remaining rebels, but their general, Cyrus, ordered them to stop.

"No one inside is to be harmed," Cyrus directed, "The rest are prisoners."

The Insurgents who rejected the surrender were forced into chains, heads down but not bowed. Their eyes stared into the ponds of red and blue, their face's reflection whole and unchanging in either.

***

Outside, the sun shimmered. It was a beautiful day. But no one paid any mind; the eyes of the nation watched only the newsreels. Reporter after reporter detailed the overwhelmingly successful offensive against the militant rebels as government officials made celebratory addresses across the country. In a single sweeping blow, the Insurgent's hidden compounds were burned and ransacked as the upper levels cheered and paraded like people freed from death row. Among the elite, however, some did not lose themselves to the wave of exuberance. They clenched their fists and gritted their teeth into smiles. Traitors that went unnoticed among the outbreak of joy.

Meanwhile, where the sun's rays did not reach, the masses in the roads stood still. Some faces, hidden by gas masks to protect them from the smog, became grim with the announcement. Other faces blinked on with a certain dullness lingering in their eyes. A few smiled all the same, content and undefeated, sharpening the blades of their hearts. One child unknowingly, instinctively, turned towards the sun she couldn't see, hidden by man-made walls. Abyss walkers were allowed no stars. Closing her eyes, though, it was as if the barriers melted away with the light burning against her eyelids, a flush of red and orange, the feeling of light tugging away at the curtains of night.

***

Levels above, in the City of Midan, an investigator filed through the marble hallway, the scrubbed floor reflecting an image of professionalism. Black hair tied in a slick bun, outfitted into a black and white suit with black leather shoes clutching the ground as she strode under the roof of bars and cells. ID tag hanging off her waist, she approached security, recalling her objective as she underwent the security scan. As part of the Instability Investigation branch, her supervisors instructed her to interview one of the Insurgents and understand their motives. What fueled their uprising, and what action was needed to prevent another? She knew her goals. Stability. Civility. Peace. These were ideals worth preserving, she thought, not some worthless attempt to rock the boat to achieve an abstract dream. Change dripped slowly from the ceiling of the cave, and she believed it was better to accept that than to petition against something immutable like gravity.

"You're good to go," the security guard said.

The investigator delved deeper into the prison.

Shouts rang through the facility and guards stalked up and

down the corridors, like pacing predators waiting for a hint of movement. Cameras craned their necks like owls. Turrets sat like tortoises. She stared at them while walking past, as if they might acknowledge her presence. The place felt rigid yet smooth, like an infinite series of squares forming a circle. Caged by the iron of the bars or the steel of falsehood, everyone inside was a prisoner, except for one. Glancing at the prisoners, the investigator felt a wave of disgust spread across her face and pass just as quickly. Painting her face with indifference, she entered the elevator and dropped into the earth.

With the crime rate continuously climbing, prisons struggled with the influx and the upper dwellers struggled with the unnerving sight of a prison joining them in the air. So, the State of Nardeban decided to dig down. In the dirt, sterile lights revealed sneaking shadows vanishing from the walls with cages built for moles and worms. Here they hid away the worst of the worst, kept out of sight and out of mind. Here lay the uncomfortable thoughts they suppressed, and the ideas that stirred fear into their hearts. Here was a place disconnected from even the abyss; what prisoners called the Void.

Some questions lingered in her mind as she slipped in and out of darkness, the weak white lights only shining on a sparse surface area. After analyzing the reports, she discovered footage from one of the army's battles against the Insurgents, and the inconsistencies rattled her. Later, the video was deleted and tagged as false, but one aspect of it concerned her. Only those who refused to surrender to the army survived. Slaughtering those who surrendered, sparing those who fought back. Perhaps they struck a deal, the investigator wondered, betraying their ideals for survival. But what if there was another purpose behind their imprisonment? By preserving the lives of those who refused to surrender, they lived on as samples to study, assigning investigators like her to pick them apart the way an epidemiologist tracks down the germ that sparks a plague. She was the doctor, though, unlike other doctors, she walked forward to meet not with her patient but with the sickness. She arrived at the cell. It was filled with a crisp darkness, barren of any bed or comfort. Everything in the cell followed regulation. The crumbly dirt walls barely rose to a height of seven feet, aching under the weight of the earth, a wall that competed with the might of Atlas. Inside, the man held his hands out in front of his face, lips parting and closing slowly as he whispered, unaware of her standing outside. Body donned with rags and scraps, hair overgrown and ratty, face gaunt and gray, he lowered his arms as she opened the door.

The air stirred as she stepped in. Involuntarily, she hesitated before going inside. Was it the cell? Was it him? The rest of the prison was kept right at the interval of cold that wouldn't hurt you, merely locking you in a state of constant discomfort with frost breathing down your back. Yet this cell was warm, chillingly so to the ice that blazed inside her. It was as if she was invited in. Without speaking, she took a seat and set down a recorder on the table.

"What's this all about?" he questioned, noting her ID badge.

"You are not to speak unless spoken to," she began, thrusting each word forward with calm precision, shrugging off her earlier inhibitions. "This is an official interview; everything you say will be recorded. Do you consent, Prisoner 04?"

He replied, "I don't have much of a choice, do I?" He didn't have the face of a prisoner. His brow stood at ease, as if unaware of the chain on his leg.

She continued, "The device will begin recording," she fiddled with the black ovaloid disk, "now." A red light brightened the cell ominously, flashing in and out.

"State your name."

"Abraham."

"Your age?"

"40."

"What was your position in the Insurgency?"

"I was a founder."

She raised her eyebrows momentarily. She kept up her questions, shooting each one like an arrow into him with the hopes she could discover what flowed inside.

"What drove you to create the Insurgency?"

His eyes danced. "I did not create it any more than a bird creates the wind it pushes against to fly. It existed before it was made and used today, and it will exist after. It is nothing but a lighthouse, to guide lost sailors home."

Mentally rolling her eyes, she said, "Describe the more recent intent behind the organization, in *real* terms this time."
"To gain liberty. To restore justice. To enact equality, abolish poverty, usurp the rich," his lip twitched into a slanted grin, "that's what you expected me to say, right? Our intent now is no different from our original one. What you think is real and what I think is real, I wager, are quite different. The Insurgency, as your lot calls it, is nothing except for an operation centered on light, to teach and grow. Not to fight,

not in the way you're liable to imagine. Now, why don't you tell me the *real* reason you're here?"

"You are to only give me answers to my questions, not to ask them."

"The first question you should be asking is about what questions you should ask."

Her spirits fell. She wasn't going to learn anything from him relating to her debrief. Still, she persevered. Something about this Insurgent sparked her curiosity. It was a whim, though she was rarely the kind of person that pursued whims. "What do you believe caused your failure?"

"What failure? I saw nothing but success. There is no success without sacrifice. In fact," he went on with his voice lighting up the room as even the red light of the recording disk appeared to dim, "The key to my success is with me right now."

Frustrated, she said, "Answer the question." He refused to speak, only passing her a glance of what seemed like pity. His eyes didn't look at her or through her; they peered within. *That's not the look of a prisoner*, she thought testily. The others knew to keep their heads down, wilting plants in a place without sun. She realized this was getting nowhere. "What motivated your illegal and dangerous acts? Why bother creating the Insurgency?"

Surprising her, he paused. Thus far for her investigation his quippy answers provided nothing. There was defiance in his quietness, a stern dignity. Now, he spoke untethered. "Let me take you back, investigator. Back to where the In- surgency was first started."

She leaned in. He went on.

"Growing up in Level 5 of Midan, no one read me any stories. There were no heroes to look up to. No villains to look down upon. Nothing fed my imagination. The future and the past might as well have been the same. I couldn't envision anything except for the moment in front of me. I was blind and hungry. That's life down in the dwellings.

"It's probably difficult for someone like you to understand, someone who has read stories, who lives up with the clouds and the stars, who doesn't need a gas mask to breathe the air you corrupted, who doesn't need to worry about the rain washing everything away. But we did. That's where I was raised, in a place bereft of power. The powerless and the powerful, me and you. A life doomed to waste away either drunk or in a jail, where your past was your present and where your present was your future.

"That was how I viewed it before. I now realize you all, as high up as you are with those glaring signs, are just as devoid of light. You, in the skies, and us, in the earth, aren't so different. We seek what you preserve, but neither of us receive what we actually need."

"What," she spat, "are you saying?"

His head tilted forward, "Tell me, are you free? Have you ever thought about what that might even mean? What if I told you that there is no difference between the levels, what if I told you that they're all one and the same?" Compassion laced his words, almost causing her to stumble in her response. The ice inside began to sweat.

Unsettled, the interrogator tried to ignore him and pushed on, "Get to the point."

"Eager, are we?" he laughed to himself and afterwards gave a small look of guilt. "I shouldn't laugh. Please, remain patient with me. You remind me of an old friend, so I hope you'll hear me out. On to the story.

"Venturing through those dumps my friends and I called home, we encountered an elderly woman. She was kind. Really kind. Something about her glowed even brighter than those city lights dangling up like stars. Whatever it was made those other lights look like shadows.

"She was a storyteller. Together, we'd visit her and listen, and those stories radiated the same brightness she did. They were hope, but they were also something more." He paused again, while the interrogator merely listened, intrigued. This was not the story she was expecting. This was not the man she was expecting.

His words flowed softly, delicately, as if he was afraid his mouth might break them, as if they carried something precious that could not be seen through the air they breathed through. "One day, she told us a different story. I watched her, for the first time, cry and cry and cry. My heart ached from her crying. The next story, she said, was real. Thousands of years ago, there was a man that was not a man, a mortal that was not a mortal. Otherworldly in character, his family garnered respect across the land, he himself the grandson of a prophet, the final prophet. However, his grandfather's teachings, like a pure river diverting into a muddy strait, grew distorted and warped, and the grandson was refused his inheritance, his right to rule. In his place, a tyrant arose. But the grandson made no grab for power. His duty was to guide. His mission focused on the hearts of the people, and his majesty and character were such that any kingship awarded to him did not elevate him, rather, he elevated the kingship itself. But the tyrant, seeking legitimacy, asked him to recognize the tyranny, to grant authority to the stolen seat. He, in an act that inspired the Insurgency, never revolted, instead stating simply, 'A person like me could never give allegiance to a person like you.' Infuriated, the despot continued his harsh rule, and the king of the hearts maintained his stance, avoiding war for he knew it only summoned tragedy to his followers." A tear slowly streamed down Abraham's face, and he cleared his throat.

"What happened next?" the interrogator asked, surprising herself. Despite herself, her guard was loosened by the melody of his recital.

"One day, a city called out to him, and destiny made its way to him. The people sent countless letters, pleading for his help and guidance. He could not refuse. So he packed up his modest belongings, and, along with his family and resolute companions, left the home of his grandfather, driven by duty. A journey of months, he stopped from city to city, preaching and warning, carrying the torch of his grandfather through the long nights before him despite knowing what was to come. He spoke of revolution, but not as we think of it. He urged for others to overthrow themselves, to battle the tyrant of the soul. The man above men moved forward. At long last, the two forces confronted each other, one seeking war, one seeking peace. One breathing hypocrisy, one bleeding freedom. In the heat of the desert, the area known as Karbala, this story both begins and ends. The king of hearts was to become the king of martyrs.

"For three days, the tyrant's army cut off the man's family and companions from water. Women and children, sons and daughters, brothers and sisters. On the tenth day of the month, the tyrant's army initiated their attack, an army of thirty thousand against a force that didn't even reach one hundred. One by one, the man watched his companions, followers whose devotion and courage were unmatched and undenied, reject his offer to flee while they could. One by one, he watched his sons and brothers go to war. As they fell in battle, he witnessed the barbarity, cut limbs, splintered bodies, and held each dying one in his arms. His followers considered his embrace to be life itself. Without urging, they fought and bled and sacrificed of their own accord, and as deep as he felt despair so, too, did he feel satisfaction in the way of God. His grief was rooted in piety and pity, and he feared not for his loss but for the loss of his enemies. He was a leader for the entirety of humanity. His heart strained from the sight, for he saw with his heart, of those who committed themselves to darkness and stumbled blindly onto his encampment, dooming themselves. His time came, Death marched closer, and soon they embraced. The women and children left behind were taken and imprisoned and disgraced. He died thirsty, not just for water but for justice. He died resisting, he died not as an aggressor but as a responder. Responding to the cries for help and the wail of inner and outer tyranny. He left behind only the prince of hearts, and the prince's survival promised the return of a Savior. One destined to return to the earth, when the gates of the heart are open.

"Inspired, we all came back and asked her to tell us his story again. Our minds were blinded by his heroism, how he never bent to the will of oppression. Each time we did, her eyes glimmered with sorrow, saying one day we would come to understand the secret of her story. She refused our request and gently turned us away."

The interrogator, too absorbed in the narrative he weaved, wordlessly let him continue. The storm within her crackled and a shining raindrop thawed from ice that gave way to the warmth of the cell.

Abraham grew thoughtful.

"It was the last day we ever saw her. When we came back the next day, she disappeared, leaving only her house behind. Some of the others even forgot she was ever there." "However," he started with his eyes flying up to meet hers, "after all this I have still told you nothing."

Engrossed in the narrative moments before, the investigator's thoughts rattled against her skull. "You told me about nothing but another failure and wasted my time here." Her once calibrated voice betrayed a slight shiver. She never heard this tale, yet it felt familiar to her. Doubt shined on her forehead.

Abraham shook his head. "Hearing this story, your type might be tempted to label it as the root of rebellion, the seed of insurrection. It is, in part. Though the battle we wage extends beyond merely Nardeban or the City of Midan. It is a battle against apathy, against the darkness of ignorance, and it is a battle for empathy, for the light of understanding. It is a war within the heart, where every day we decide which side of the battlefield we're on through either our forgetfulness or remembrance."

"What does that mean? I don't understand how what you're saying has anything to do with what pushed the Insurgency forward. What exactly are you trying to tell me?," the investigator asked. She was the interrogator, she was here for answers, answers she hadn't anticipated wanting.

"You call me an insurgent. I am not. I am a revolutionary. You tell me I failed. I have not. I am the victor in ways you cannot understand. You ask what motivates me. I needed nothing but this. Those of us who later understood her words, we joined an existing revolution, a timeless cycle of loss and fulfillment. There is a strength in standing, in sacrificing, in struggling and it can never be in vain. There is something more than what you can ever hope to see with those eyes of yours." He rose from his seat and in that moment she understood why the Insurgency caused such an uproar, unlike the other resistances before it. He spoke boldly, untainted by anger, and the whole cell seemed to blaze with him. She hated it. She felt drawn to it.

"Call me Sisyphus, but at least I know which boulder I'm rolling and which mountain I'm on. And you? What are you fighting for? To subjugate the denizens of Level 5?" His words were fierce but he spoke them with a gentle urgency. The investigator could handle being yelled at in tough cases; this was different.

"How dare you? I'm protecting my city from rabble rousers like you. Everything in Midan, everything in Nardeban all stands on one leg. Stop trying to knock it over just because *your type* believes they can take a step forward."

"Do you think you're preserving some peace? Did you consider what kind of peace you help force everyone else to live under? You might not like what I'm saying, but you can hear me. I see it in your eyes."

"That's enough. Take a seat," she responded icily. Her pride pulled back her tongue from the urge to question him for more. Cruelty crushed curiosity. She tried to shake off its lingering traces but they clung to her like rain. Rain that seeped through the soil, that touched the veins of the earth.

"I haven't told you everything. There are other stories. They say history moves in cycles. By learning the story of another, it is with the hope that we uncover the stages of our own."

"What makes you think I need to know anything else about you and your rebel group?" she snapped back, shocking herself. It was one final defensive to ward off his words.

A chuckle broke loose from Abraham's lips. "I have no reason to tell you for my own sake. Your superiors will be interested, and I have nothing left to hide. It's all in your favor, and there is much I wish to tell you. I do have one condition, though."

"What is it?" she asked.

"Will you tell me your name?

She glared at him, bitter at his insolence towards her and resentful at her own confusion from his words. "I am your interrogator, that is all you need to know."

His face stiffened, "Are you?"

She only replied, "We'll meet again next week." But she found herself unwilling to move just yet, as something pulled on her to ask one final question, even after she shut the recording disk off, leaving the room pitch black.

Seconds of silence rolled into minutes until finally she spoke, "Does this story have a name?"

Solemnly, he said, "The Tragedy at Karbala."

***

Captain Jonah sat across from the Supervisor whose manner, as always, remained both alert and relaxed, like a panther patiently tracking its hunt. He fidgeted awkwardly, waiting for her to acknowledge his presence. Only her back faced him as her eyes remained focused on the window.

The office was embellished with achievements, gold-tinted certificates lining the standard gray walls and the floor tiled with a shining black granite that consumed any shadow unlucky enough to fall on its vicinity. Her desk betrayed nothing, bearing only a simple lamp and some sort of ring box. All interest and detail were drained from its design; it existed hoping to never be noticed, calculated austerity. Jonah sat and looked forward furtively where to either side of the Supervisor were bookshelves filled with histories of the world and records on past cases the Instability Investigative branch dealt with.

They're essential to our work, she told him at their first private meeting. Regular people were fickle and the rebellious ones were predictable. The science of destroying motivation was not lost on her.

The view outside consumed her, though it was only cracked stone with weeds weaseling their way to the surface, dotted with waste and smothered in smog normal to the polluted depths. She personally asked to station her stays here, in the barren wastelands of Midan.

Suddenly, her raven hair flew behind her and she posed to Jonah, "Can you imagine anyone calling this beautiful?"

Uncertain, he replied, "No, ma'am," fingers thrumming against his lap. He wanted to be in and out as quickly as possible.

Her shadowed glare pinned him to the seat, asking, "How goes our interrogator?" Noting his slight confusion, she added, " The one assigned to Prisoner 04."

He cleared his throat. "Nothing out of the ordinary in the report Miss." Spying for an opportunity, he put forward a question, as gingerly as one might touch a porcupine, "Is there anything we should be worried about?"

The shadowed glare loosened, replaced by a small smile, "No, there's nothing at all to fear; in fact, this is the end of our meeting."

Suppressing a look of relief, Jonah nodded and headed for the door, but the Supervisor's voice called out to him, "Next time, I'd like a copy of the recording disc. For every meeting, naturally."

Next time? He sighed internally. Well, it would be a good chance for him to take a listen to some of those recordings too. Might make for a good podcast. "Of course Miss, have a good day," he responded while slipping on his gas mask.

***

The city of Midan, like its neighbors and cousins through the continent, was sliced into steps. With each step up, one approached opulence, freedom from the infested air below. With each step down, there was decay— and there were the forgotten. The glowing skyline above built itself upon the destitute and the ruins and the past. All suffocated in their own way. The first from the air, the second from the darkness, and the third from the future.

Almost one week ago the investigator spoke to that man, Prisoner 04, Abraham. The story he told her, the Tragedy at Karbala, she felt it within her. It pulsed like a living heart and it ignited an urge to visit the surface world, the depths of Midan. Her hands splayed across the glass of Charon's Boat, the elevator that took one down through the Levels, as it descended. Before her, she witnessed the towering scapes of her home, a shower of light in a world quickly growing dim. The sight took her breath away each time. The soaring spires curled up into the air like vines. What she was seeing now was salvation, it had to be. Her loose fingers wrung themselves into a fist, this was the place she had known all her life, that she sought to protect and preserve. Yet, his words could not leave her. An epitaph, thousands of years old, made a denizen of the deep long to collapse what she raised, to raze what was a part of her. And to discover whatever lay beneath.

The scene shifted. She fell faster and faster, cradled in the elevator, and outside the image warped from the maze of flying roads and castles in the sky to ramshackle huddles and coughing clouds chained to the earth. Her fingers gently rolled open once again, the lines of the interrogator's palm carving a path of frustration. Her city was built on a hill of trash. He called the Insurgency a lighthouse. He brushed off its role in merely fixing the disgusting state of the depths. If that was all, then she would understand. Anyone would. But there was something else. Something more. It scared her, it made her question what she loved. She reflected on what endears someone towards something, what qualities produce love. She never thought about things that way before.

The Boat of Charon came to an abrupt stop, and the interrogator, with her face shielded, walked outside. The earth crumbled beneath her footsteps, powderizing from the slightest touch and rustling up like sand. Like a desert.

The familiar embrace of the sun, its hug of warmth, was gone down here. Instead, a cold wall of fog blocked the sky and the land. It reminded her of the Void, the prison, but here the entire world was the cell. But Abraham thought this abyss was no different from the upper levels.

She walked, feeling the weight of a dream blanket over her mind. Her steps wound up dancing to the song of the land, humming and entranced.

Her concentration dissolved. At first, she thought the noises came from the crickets. She wasn't used to them, or any of the sounds of 'nature' for that matter. The investigator's ears were attuned to the robust floating metropolis now miles above her, not the groans and aches of land untouched by iron and steel.

She realized they were voices. She strained her eyes to see past the smudge of white surrounding her to no avail but still the voices pestered on. In a life of listening to instructions, she somehow found herself here on her own accord, for reasons she couldn't understand. She hoped something from this abyss would guide her, something that could explain *him*.

One of the voices grew louder, and it seemed to penetrate the fog.

"I can bear this no longer."

It was the voice of a man, it was shaking and breaking, filled with regret of a sin from long ago. Immediately, the interrogator shot her head in the direction of the sound, jogging forward.

"I… the river…," his words grew fainter, farther, darker. She didn't know who it was and her cries didn't reach him, so she finally ran and ran until she was greeted by the breath of a river, its mist distinct from the tendrils of fog grasped at her legs, refusing to let her go. The weight of the world she knew pulled against her, and the frost within her heart tried to seal itself, the cracks were still thin and translucent, there was a chance to stay away, to keep everything the same—but a part of her refused. The ice shrieked as a tear thawed from her eye, the frost wailed as it lost its grip on her, the fog of lies trembled as she sought the truth. She needed to understand. She needed to *see*.

After what felt like an eternity, like her entire life flowed past her, she sprinted through the river bed chasing the breath of a dead man. The land remembered him, even this powdery earth.

Again, she caught a taste of his voice, drenched in dread and soaked in sorrow.

"I beseech you upon my hands and knees..."

The wind drifted it upstream and the interrogator's legs shot against the ground, hand unknowingly reaching forward, yelling for any response to the warm spray of mist.

"I am responsible for your suffering. It is I who deprived you, who blocked your way."

Another man spoke, one whose sound was both sweet and sorrowful. It gathered her attention like honey, as he responded, "It is only you who has deprived yourself, only you who blocked your own way to me. But you are here."

"I do not know if you can forgive me. How can I ever live knowing I was the one who hurt you? The one who saddened your holy mother?" The voice lashed itself with a guilt that felt like it destroyed the world. A bitter shame filled that tongue and made it retch at its own wickedness.

This grief poured into her, through the mist she could not see through, but felt as if it was closer to her than her own breath, closer to the sun than its own light. Few ever questioned if they were the villain. Few ever questioned their role in history, whether they would side with the righteous or with the wicked. They needed to. Goodness was not an assumption, purity was not a given. It was a fruit that took time to cultivate, roots to care for.

"Come to me. Stand with me. Fight for me. Be as your mother named you. Be free."

The investigator stumbled to a halt, forced to bend over and catch her breath yet the tiredness slipped through her. She made it, this is where the sounds led her to. She raised her head and saw nothing. There was nothing but a bird, now frightened off by her approach, soaring into the sky. Lightning tore through the clouds, and its flash illuminated her reflection even in the rushing river. Then, she stooped over and cried, from a despair she could not name and an anguish she could not find. Her heart's ice was driven through by a double forked flame, and it flowed like the stream in which she deposited her tears.

***

Abraham kept his head down as she opened the cell door.

"I… I want you to tell me the stories you mentioned," she requested, free from the coldness once blazing through her.

He responded simply. "Of course."

From that day onwards, for four months the interrogator visited Abraham. Her ambition tempered into patience, her fears gave way to understanding, and her heart blinked like one awoken from a deep dream. Her hatred of the Insurgency, her distaste of Abraham, these, too, transformed.

She brought with her small amenities for Abraham, bottled relief in a prison like the Void. Gestures of respect. But what refreshed him, and her, most were their conversations.

"The Insurgency's original goal was never focused on purely striking back against the hovering citadels. Unlike the rebellions of the past, our goals were never defined through the lens of our oppressor; we didn't desire the same thing they desired. Our message extended beyond the divides between those in the sky or of the earth— to God, they were one and the same without light. Everyone was forgetting and trying to forget, either with the luxuries of the top or the intoxicating dejection of the bottom. They searched for glory in gems that were dust and sought liberty in shiny chains." She raised an eyebrow, one question bursting free from her mind. "Why did you say you wanted revolution then?" Pushing back his tattered hair with one hand, he replied, "Because I do want revolution. Not just the revolution of a society. The revolution of truth against falsehood, a revolution of collective remembrance. A revolution that takes place inside individuals. That is the only way those from below or from above will ever be able to climb to the light. There is no greater sin than to forget where we came from." The investigator swiveled her head to the ground, thinking. Many strings weaved the cloth of her life, strings of career and ambition, strings of desire for justice and peace. It felt like the surface was eroding away, dust to the wind of light whose love enveloped and guided her. She never quite loved Nardeban, she witnessed its flaws everyday. But its cold fingers shaped her in ways she never realized, until the justice she sought was as much Nardeban's product as its oppressions.

"And," Abraham finished, "there is no greater worship than to remember who we are."

***

Weeks passed as she updated and passed on her recording disk to her employers over the interviews, and one day she was called back to the Instability Investigations branch.

A jingle from her holophone led her to report back to her supervisor, and she went with uncharacteristic eagerness through the hallway, her coordinated steps now threatening to morph into a speed walk.

She set foot into his office and Captain Jonah wasted no time with his instructions. "You need to destroy the recording disk immediately." The investigator's expression spoke before she could.

"I understand that you've worked on this case for a long time, but it's out of our control," he said, "the higher ups shut down the investigation into the Insurgency." Jonah looked confused himself.

"This can't be right, Captain, isn't there anything-" A look from Jonah cut her off.

"One last thing before you go. One of the higher ups wants to meet with you to discuss a promotion. You can meet with her down in Level 5, I'll upload the directions to your ho-lotech. The meeting is set for five days from now; trust me, don't be late. It's… the Supervisor."

The interrogator barely registered his words, tossing them aside for her real desire. "Is there any way I can request more interviews with Abraham at least? I think these discussions can prove fruitful for the branch, it gives a direct look into rebel operations…" She fluttered out excuse after excuse that she held no faith in, determined to get another chance to meet with Abraham to continue their sessions, to learn more about herself and, through that, to learn more about the world. Those few months seemed to carry the weight of lifetimes.

After letting her rattle off a litany of possible projects and their purposes, Jonah finally replied, "There's no point. His execution, along with the rest of the remaining Insurgent prisoners, is set for just under a week for now. I won't authorize any more meetings."

Stunned, she exited the office with silence filling her lungs. Her limbs slowly unlocked and mechanically she headed down to the incinerator. She took the stairs, her feet moving on their own accord as she overheard her colleagues discussing the recent news. Rumors of a fractured Insurgency, riots rolling through cities, the mass dispatchment of law enforcement to overwhelmingly suppress the outcry. The cry of a mission left unfinished.

Descending from floor to floor, her thoughts churned. What in the recording incited its destruction? It should prove useful to them. Beyond that, they planned to kill the Insurgents. That part shouldn't have shocked her. Not long before they eliminated most of the Insurgency's ranks, it only made sense to finish off the surviving few once their purpose was fulfilled. But what purpose? After all, they wanted to destroy the recordings. Her logic grappled with a festering feeling of vague wrongness.

She stood before the incinerator. In her hands, she held the black disk. Each step felt momentous, crashing against the ground as she felt that word in her mind once again. Karbala. Memory. She dropped the disk.

The flames gulped greedily at the deposited darkness. There was nothing more for her to learn from them. The inferno crackled as the recording turned on one last time.

"Goodbye… Zulayka." It was Abraham's voice.

She remembered that session. It was the first time she had ever told him her name. A rose of flames erupted in her heart, its petals of embers burning gentle tears of smoke. The fire burned away its stains and cracks, scorching through the suffocating veils with its hunger to finally breathe the pure air. The fire incinerated the strings of ignorance woven into a deep sheet of sleep, unraveling a song whose tune she always knew and freeing its words from its dusty corner. The song colored the world with its music, and the world colored the song, forming an orchestra of a hundred voices blurring into one. When she climbed back up, each step whispered back to her, the walls relieved themselves of their burden and told her their secrets, the trees rustled in their secret language of falling leaves, the people spoke to her without speaking as their faces were revealed. The skin of the fruit gives way to the flesh lying underneath, the world of its surface as only a barrier to the depths of its sweetness.

The Drowning Feather

The Drowning Feather

From You, 2000 Years Ago

When they released each other, the night timidly cast its shade. The moon struggled to hide its glowing scars under the horizon, the stars tried to drag themselves back to their hiding places, the darkness writhed in its leash as it swept over the sand. Time sighed and performed its duty, the one entrusted to it before the first of days, the reason for its existence.

The sister, too, unwillingly retreated from her brother, the crownless king who returned to his knights. In reverence to his heavenly steps that graced the earth, the army of faith quieted, tasting his presence for the last time.

All of humanity, though, stood in that tent. And all of humanity listened to his words.

"Blow out your candles, please," he said.

They obeyed. The night wrapped itself around them, the light cloaked within them simmered silently.

"Those of you who wish to leave, I will hold no grudge against you. Leave under the cover of the dark."

Not one moved.

The rest of humanity hidden in the tent, the ones who lived before, the ones destined to be born, were not so unanimous.

***

Zulayka arrived at the Supervisor's office with the news of Abraham's coming execution lingering over her. One more day and his life would end. Another feather smashed to the ground, robbed of its graceful landing. Gingerly, she removed her gas mask, nose twitching at the odorless space. The smell of nothing permeated the ventilated room, scrubbed clean against the shining darkness of the tiles beneath her feet, studded with tiny glowing stars. It was like stepping into the night.

The Instability Investigation branch held its cards tightly to its chest, with its numbers out on the field to gather information, the Jacks and Queens and Kings shut up in offices and research stations. Their Ace was the Supervisor. News of her work traveled in hushed tones, spoken in words unsaid whenever a rebel base was uncovered, whenever an insurgent compound met its end. Like a spider laying its web, the Supervisor flew throughout the system. Her victories studded the wall in gold frames hung onto gray walls.

"Welcome, interrogator. Take a seat."

Her voice sliced through Zulayka's thoughts, leaving only unease.

"I have come as requested, Miss…," she waited for the Supervisor to offer up a name, and was left with none.

"You should already know that this interview is about your promotion, Zulayka," stating the interrogator's name to her, as if to taunt Zulayka's earlier attempt at receiving one. "Your recent experiences make you uniquely suited to the task I am to entrust to you. That is, if you accept," she spoke measuredly.

"I understand," Zulayka responded with distrust at the edge of her lips. This woman, she realized, put the Insurgents to death. There was a glee in the otherwise polished air.

"It was I who assigned you to Prisoner 04." The Supervisor paused, analyzing Zulayka's reactions with her wood brown eyes, like a sheet of unfeathered branches creeping over the sky. "I have listened to your conversations with him. But he has not been truthful to you. He didn't tell you everything that you need to know. So, let me tell you the true story of the Insurgency, and why our paths are one, Zulayka." Noticing Zulayka tense up, the Supervisor let out a brief chuckle.

"Relax, and listen."

***

"Rabia!"

The girl bounding forward moments ago impatiently bounced back at the sound of her father's voice. A dulled red scarf rested on her head. With careful fingers, her dad attached her gas mask to her face. His hands were withered from a fatigue beyond his age. Rabia fidgeted and waited and peeked her head behind her, seeing all her friends slowly make their way through the wastelands of Midan, slipping betwixt the fog.

With a click, her father grinned, "All done!" Flashing him an appreciative smile, Rabia turned around and screamed, "Wait for me!," as she charged into the mist.

The air was thick with grime while the earth choked from the endless debris. A garish gray sky stared down at the land, acidic sympathy spilling from its eyes. Plastic and metal tore holes through its almost-but-not-quite silver flesh. Sometimes, the ceiling above cracked open, and their young eyes bore witness to white lights birthed from black oil, buildings whose size escaped their understanding. This was Level 5 of the city of Midan, the furthest below.

The abyss children wandered here, steps quick with childish excitement. They dug up treasures from the trash, exploring the heaps of rubble that whispered and groaned of a battle from long ago with every shift in its lumbering mass. Rummaging through the trash sent a soft shockwave buzzing through the piles of rubbish, and it breathed in the crashes and shifts of its heaving chest.

There were five of them that day. Along with Rabia, there was Abe, the youngest of the group, his brother Isaac, and the two other girls, Naamah and Zahra, who bounded excitedly into Rabia's arms.

"Don't be so slow!," Abe yelled, pushing Naamah to the side and charging forward. An exasperated Isaac quickly apologized on his brother's behalf, helping Naamah up as Zahra and Abe raced each other to the clearest field for miles, their designated location for tag.

"That kid's a brat," Naamah replied, annoyed. Though she pitied Isaac for having to keep up with him.

Rabia nodded, agreeing with her. Abe was no good, and too much in a hurry for his own good or for anyone else's. "He'll never make it to the higher levels," she stated haughtily. Her father's stories of the upper levels stood at the forefront of her mind. A place where they banished the dark of the night, where everyone could have sweets whenever they wanted, and so much more. She had sworn to reach those heights.

"He's still young, he's not even 8 yet," Isaac protested with a small smile. "One day, you'll see. He just needs some direction. Give him a chance."

Rabia glanced at him sympathetically. She found the idea

unimaginable. She was the same age as Abe but not even half as infuriating. Abe was lucky to have such a mature brother. She couldn't help but feel bad for him, though. Abe and his brother were orphans.

They stopped. The brown bush in front of them rustled menacingly, and Isaac took a step back in hesitation.

"What do you guys think that was?" he asked, with a thinly veiled attempt at apathy.

"Scaredy-cat," Naamah teased, and she walked forward, only to be tackled by a trashbag-cloaked shape ramming her into the ground.

"Naamah!," Isaac shouted, fear freezing his feet in place. Hearing a shifting behind him, Isaac barely had time to turn his head around before whatever lay in wait attacked him.

"Boo!" Abe yelled, satisfied with his brother's signature look of 'I'm going to die.'

A chorus of giggles broke out, with Naamah completely unfazed by Zahra's leap at her while Isaac tried to laugh it off. Rabia high-fived Zahra as they shared a pair of roguish smiles.

The five children walked together to the field, with Rabia and Zahra holding hands. After countless matches of rock, paper, scissors, and with some cheating on the part of Zahra ("Of course I can use a finger gun!," she had said indignantly), a pouty Rabia was chosen as the first seeker for hide and seek.

"Ten, nine, eight…," she counted loudly, and quickly, as she heard the others run off and strained to tell where they were going. There were too many places to hide when no one was looking for you. "Seven, six—" Rabia was cut off by a loud crash. It was the Boat of Charon, carrying someone far away from the bubble of her life. She hated it. It was a sore reminder for a bruise that would never heal. Life in Level 5 wasn't all fun and games. "Five, four…," she resumed, jealousy gripping her tongue. Those people who rose through the levels, they had everything. Not her. Not her father. He was sick, and growing sicker. When she watched him come home, a deep fury clawed inside her, indignant at the unfairness of the world. She continued with, "three, two…" But her mind bubbled up with memories of her friends, of Zahra, and Rabia shook the feelings off. One day, she would make it to the upper levels, and everything would turn out for the better. She took a deep breath, and, "One! Ready or not, here I come!" A dust storm quaked in her wake as she sped off.

***

"Gotcha!"

A nervous Isaac approached Rabia, standing by the recently found Naamah and Zahra.

"What's wrong, Isaac?," Naamah asked with concern as she restricted Zahra from running off and hiding again.

"It's Abe, I can't find him anywhere. He was with me and then it was like he vanished," Isaac's words were fast and slurred with worry. "We need to go find him."

With a sneer, Rabia declared, "Good riddance!" A glare from Naamah made her immediately stop talking. Isaac had no one but Abe, and Abe had no one but Isaac. She awkwardly glanced at the ground, apologetic.

Hours crept alongside a sunset they couldn't see as the congested sky glowed a fiery dark orange. Despair dragged down Isaac's back, his eyes solemn. The group wandered far from the clear field, and it was becoming too dark for them to return home.

"I'm sorry, I didn't want it to take this long, I don't know where he is—" Isaac paused abruptly, his gaze entangled by something on the horizon.

Rabia turned around and saw a ramshackle house, topped with metal scrap and strung together by loose rods and wire. For a home down in the depths, it was spacious with its metallic body jutting out to the sides and narrowing, like a tent made for robots. There weren't any down here, though. What really shocked her, and the rest of them, was the light emanating from the structure. No, that wasn't right. The lights on the house were like any other, using old-fashioned light bulbs with cracks and breaks riveting through them. Yet, these rays seemed to reach them, a calm green shine without shadow.

"We should check if Abe is there," young Zahra suggested, her voice weary and anxious. Isaac stormed ahead with the girls following closely behind.

But they didn't have to search for long, as a wily Abe sprung forward at them when they approached the entrance in bewilderment.

"Where have you been this entire time? Do you know how long we've spent searching for you?," Isaac shot out, his fear kindling into fury. Abe gulped, facing the relentless stare head on.

"I sorta got lost… I thought the best way to hide would

be to run away as far as possible, but that didn't go exactly to plan." Seeing his brother's unchanging expression, Abe quickly addressed everyone, including a sniffling Zahra, "Sorry that I didn't come back and that all of you kept looking for me. No worries, though, because I'm completely fine! In fact, there's someone I want all of you to meet." Abe called for someone in the dwelling, and whipped his head back around excitedly. "She tells the best stories!"

The door behind him swung open, and an aging hooded woman exited, leaning on an intricately carved cane. Her hands were browned from the sun, and only the shadows draping from her cloak hid the secret gleam of her face of written wrinkles. Two valleys distinctly emerged, tracing down a canal where tears once trailed down to parched lips. She smiled at the youth before her, each of them buckling under its impact, the weight of the love from someone they had never met and a love unlike what they experienced from anyone they had met before.

"These must be your friends, young man, and your brother," she spoke, and Abe nodded approvingly. The woman turned towards Isaac. "I understand your worry for your brother, but you mustn't impose your fear for him onto him. Treasure your brother, and nurture him," despondency colored her words as she remembered something. "The best nurturing comes from example. Refine yourself and you will find that he will respond in kind."

Her pure care for his interest splashed against his ears like cold water, surprised by their chilling warmth. "I will," he responded, the honey of her words transforming into the iron of his new resolve. The lady's eyes twinkled at this. "Before you all enter my tent so you get a good rest, why don't you all tell me your names?"

Isaac suppressed some untold sorrow from escaping his vision, the elderly lady's voice evoking some long forgotten memory, uncovering a wound he never bled. He resisted the tug of melancholy.

"My name is Isaac," he replied first, quietly, almost reverently, his senses pushing against the threshold of an awareness he couldn't yet grasp, eyes blinking against the light like one nudged awake from a deep slumber.

"Well, you can call me Naamah."

"Me next! I'm Zahra!"

"I forgot to tell you my name earlier! My name's Abe… I mean, Abraham," he corrected. Rabia glanced over, it was strange for Abe to ever go by his true name. But the woman smiled at this.

Looking back at the woman, Rabia cleared her throat.
"And I am Rabia."

Suddenly, the elderly woman fixed her attention on Rabia. "You want to go to the upper levels." It was a statement, not a question.

Unnerved, Rabia could only nod.

"Guard your dreams carefully, lest they wander into nightmares. Your love leads you to your desire. If you desire the same things as your subjugators, then what does that mean about your love?" Her look swept through the group. "That goes for all of you." A soft silence passed over them. "Why don't you all come in now?" she asked.

They accepted and entered the green light.

***

"You… you knew Abraham?" Zulayka asked, unable to mask the shock from her voice. Rabia, now the Supervisor, ignored her.

She continued gazing out her window, her specially requested office down in Level 5, in that same iron tent she entered all those years ago.

"Keep quiet till you finish hearing what I have to say. Your promotion relies on it. As does much else."

Her back was still turned away so she couldn't see Zulayka's reaction, but Zulayka refused to speak, unimpressed. The woman, the once Rabia, wondered if wrinkles were like paths. Time itself carved into our skin, a record that we could no longer read, a language we had forgotten. On her palm, she saw a fork. She narrowed her sight onto her thumb, its fingerprint was a spiral steering off to a sentence without a period. But spirals can go either way. One can spiral out, towards infinity, or spiral in, into nothingness. These were the signs she was taught to penetrate, an unlived memory that played out before her. The day she decided her destiny drifted back to her while the faint reflection in her window locked eyes with her. A few blinks later, and no reflection remained.

"Now, as I was saying…"

***

The match that was struck that day ignited their souls. Years after their fateful encounter, Isaac and the others founded the Insurgency, originally known simply as the Revolution. Its compounds grew to encompass Level 5s across Nardeban. So much had changed, but the five of them remained together, bonded by the light they witnessed that day. "We're going to create a lighthouse, a beacon right here in the pit of darkness," Isaac declared, his voice reverberating off the recently refurbished walls of the base, singing as clear as steel. A ragged crowd stood before him, eyes kindling. "A brilliant wish for those crashing against the waves, blinded by flashes of lightning and siren songs. A chance for those adrift to return ashore. They say in the legends of the past that there were whole skies of birds sweeping the air, moving by instinct, and moving together, towards home. How do they know which way to turn? How do they know it every time, without fail? They look not to the horizon, or down to the sea, or up at the clouds. Whatever they need to see remains within." Fists raised to the steel clouds.

And so it went. Those days marched by with hope, and the movement seemed only to expand. Rabia was there for all of it, alongside Naamah, Zahra, and Abraham, all diligently working towards the same goal, back then. Rabia was propelled along by her father's passing, stricken by avoidable illness. A seed of vengeance was planted, petalled weeds rooted in a new quest: to defend those she loved from Nardeban, to reach the opulence the upper levelers stole for themselves. The access to the medicine she needed for her father, the access to so much else that could improve their lives, this was at the heart of Rabia's revolution. Their progress did not go unnoticed.

The state of Nardeban and its leader, Bliss, were no stranger to "fissures," the term given to underground resistance from the lower levels. They happened every few decades, and they were quickly snuffed out. Not by force, but through the natural erosion of despair. The fickle justice these forces sought crumbled, and when it inevitably did so too did the resistance itself crumble. Nardeban knew this world was one where they held all the cards, secured every advantage, and cornered every piece. All the resources rested within their hands. If one's yearning for freedom came from a fear about usurping Nardeban, then their doom awaited them like the night.

The Revolution was another matter. It blindsided Nardeban with its ferocity and endurance. The flame that always sputtered out now burned on, and its smoke penetrated the Levels, all the way to the top and beyond. Something needed to be done. Bliss set a new project into motion, one born as a whisper and soon to be heard as a scream. A special operations branch, an investigative unit designed specifically to quell these fissures, to roughly rock the earth back into its forgetful sleep.

Wherever they sensed a rumble, they sent their agents, and no land stirred more than Midan. When a land is destroyed, razed to the ground, left with nothing but its ghosts and stones, it begins to recover. It always attempts to recover. The first step in this recovery starts with the lichen, small and moss-like organisms that riddle themselves along the rocks, the gravestones of the trees and the birds and the seeds. With painstaking ease, its green grassy teeth nibble on the gray pebbled darkness. The rock gives way, and the lichen spreads, on and on. The land is reborn, its soil ripe and overflowing as the seeds return. With time, patience, and stability, the stunning color tears free from the stones.

That's why that nameless agency trained itself to identify and destroy the lichen, to guard the memories that they themselves had forgotten. They decided it was time to act. Their thirst produced fire.

Surely, the just cannot tolerate the unjust, and the unjust cannot tolerate the just.

***

A boom. A crash. A silence. The compound's door shot open and pandemonium stalked the hallways with bullets whistling their deadly tune through the air. The Revolutionaries scrambled, as Nardeban's soldiers forced their way in. Naamah ran and dodged her way to Isaac in his study, exchanging looks of fear.

"We need to get everyone out of here," they spoke in unison, splitting up. Their voices, familiar and urgent, guided the Revolutionaries underground where they fanned out into the tunnels sprawling beneath the building. Abraham darted his way towards Isaac, while Naamah used their few precious minutes to seek out Rabia and Zahra; the two were inseparable, their bond only strengthened as the years flowed into it.

She found them.

Before the attack, Zahra and Rabia were stationed outside, talking with some of the others. Neither of them were children any longer, and the two led the others inside.

Naamah found Zahra in Rabia's arms, the same arms she used to hug Zahra, to take turns carrying Zahra back home when it was dark out. The sister to her soul, the younger one she always checked up on, that she strived to keep safe. What would happen to those laughs of hers when there was no breath for them to come through? A poisoned seed bloomed in Rabia's heart, its venom whispering growth into weeds.

"They started too early. Zahra was on her way back after checking to see if anyone else was outside. We tried to ask for help, but… No one came. Not one of them. Can you believe that, Naamah? I had just gotten in before her, I watched them, they…"

Rabia's voice was hollow, a dull pain echoing from her throat that pulsed in each word. Sorrow is separation. You must remember this. But separation from what?

Naamah knelt down and brought Rabia into her arms, staying still for moments that felt like an eternity. A quiet, toxic rain started. Naamah brought her cloak over Rabia. Gently, Naamah whispered, "We have to go," with tears shining in her eyes.

Together, the two snuck back and escaped through the tunnels, the earthquaking footsteps of dread above slowly fading in the distance. When they resurfaced, a grim-faced Abraham awaited them at the top of the stops, his expression no longer that of a boy, but unbroken.

"Where's…," his voice trailed off.

His softened brown eyes glowed with a sorrowful sympathy, finally catching the sight of red on Rabia. They, too, now saw it on him. He willed his anguish inside.

"Is Isaac alright?," Naamah asked quietly.

"For now. I'll take you to him."

Isaac sat on a rough tan tarp, leaning against some of the supplies they smuggled. Though his body was hidden by a blanket, the pain on his face made the situation clear. But that was nothing compared to the grief when he heard of Zahra.

"How did they find out about us?" The other's heads turned

in surprise at Rabia, whose frigid lips were shattered open by a wind of cold that blew from her lungs. Its frost made Isaac wince. He said nothing.

She stared at him, her voice raw with rage. "There must be traitors among the survivors here, Isaac. People who tipped Nardeban off about us."

Tired, Isaac said, "You may very well be correct."

"Are these the same *abyss walkers*," that name lashed out like a whip, "who are supposed to hold nobility within them?"

"A shadow isn't a good reason to start doubting the light."

"How far deep is this goodness, exactly? We've spent years, decades on this project of yours, only to lose Zahra. If that's the product, then what does any of this mean?"

Isaac answered calmly, with a deep certainty. "Nardeban has never taken anything from us. They never can. We have lost nothing, nothing that we won't get back." Raising his gaze to meet hers, he went on, "We are all from the same source, and we will all return there."

"I've heard that enough times. Once was more than enough. Why can't we just be together here and now?" Rabia snarled, interrupted by her own tears.

Isaac gazed at her sadly. "Right now, our response is to continue learning, teaching, and raising those around us. You were once among the lost. Do not lose faith in what remains inside. Don't allow your tragedy to draw you into a far deeper one." He broke out into a fit of bloodied coughing, and Rabia seized it as an advantage.

"All those years ago, we were taught to better ourselves, then to act to better our world. But after all this time, I realize that isn't possible. When Zahra and I were out there trying to save the others' lives, not one rose to help us. They fled. They left her to die. We can't keep going this way, going your way. I followed you all the way here, learned from you, respected you, but we need more." Her words picked up pace, snowballing with conviction. "What's clear to me is that none of us are special. We never were. We were born down in these dumps, destined to stay in it. We tried to fight back, didn't we?" Strained, Rabia screamed with tears streaming down her face. "And we lost. We lost so much. That Revolution you wanted is impossible. Level 5 can't stand up on its own. Look at these people. Maybe you were special Isaac, but that doesn't mean the rest of us are." Revolutionaries listening in from the sidelines shifted awkwardly.

Isaac's head dipped down in disappointment, breaking their stare. "Despair is the only poison that can kill you, Rabia. If what you say is true, that we are truly guided, then our purpose is to uplift everyone, to pass on the knowledge that was passed on to us. Or have you forgotten? Do not let your affection for Zahra or for us blind you from what ought to be the true object of your affection. Risk and sacrifice are part and parcel of our duty. And that duty, those ideals go above everything else. That is what it means to have faith. No matter what happens to us."

Rabia turned around, her shadow looming larger than ever before.

"So you will do nothing?"

"Please, Rabia."

"Don't you realize that what happened to Zahra is exactly like what happened to my father? If we abandoned this pursuit, focused on what's important, and reached the upper levels on our own like we wanted to do in the beginning, I could've saved him, and we could've saved her. The resources in our hands from Nardeban, the ability to actually help those around us. That's more important than any of these lessons to people who can't listen. A traitor ratted us out now and we survived, but what about next time? You're not just following the wrong path, Isaac, you're going to lead all of these people to their deaths, the ones still ridiculous enough to follow you after this. They're the poisoned ones."

"Please, take time to reflect—"

"And you two? You agree with him too? After what you saw happened to Zahra? After knowing what's going to happen to him?"

"Rabia…" Naamah began, faltering. Abraham looked away.

"Then… then, die here for all I care. From this day onwards, I'll do everything in my power to make sure you don't have your way." She began to walk away. Behind her Abraham rose, ready to speak and run after her, but Isaac held his hand and pulled him back. Her blindfold was already tied.

***

"That's when I found my way to the upper levels of Midan. I schemed and I hid and I sowed my chaos where I could. I was aimless. But then I was caught by Nardeban. By Leader Bliss himself. Once he realized who I was, however, the chips fell into my hands. I held something he wanted, and he held the keys for what I wanted. The ideology that drove the Insurgency, that belief in the light of others, that is what I seek to destroy. That thoughtless idealism… I know you hate it too. I have been keeping my on you for quite some time, Zulayka. Listen. The story that woman told us, the tragedy of Karbala, foretold the mistakes they were making. Anyone who follows that path is doomed to the same end— annihilation. The Insurgents thought that what they were doing was following the path of that man from the story, the man who sacrificed everything; but they're wrong, and you know that Zulayka. I am the only one who realizes what's important, the elevation and protection of those who truly are able to improve themselves, unlike everyone else. You, Zulayka, are one of the few who I recognized as being capable of that. Eventually, I climbed my way to the top, to the lights of a Level I never even imagined, and realized my old name was worthless. To envision the future, I needed to become someone new. For my new goal, I needed to gain Bliss' trust, to pulverize the remains of the group Isaac created.

"More and more, he led people astray, even after his death. Up until the very end, he still thought he was winning." Zulayka remained silent, the winds of her thought slicing ribbons through her mind's sky. The woman without a name, meanwhile, seemed to wriggle in rage, humming with the simmering fury of a furnace. "I became the Supervisor, traveling across the state, from Level to Level, weaving discord among the ranks of the Revolution wherever I could. I discovered there were plenty who were like me. Plenty who desired the truth, who knew that we needed to act. But trust must be earned. For those who sided with me in the Insurgency, they have been gifted wonders beyond their belief, more than they could ever have achieved in rebellion. " She clenched her fists and smoke vented from her jaws, "The peace Isaac tried to foster from within… it can only be achieved by striking peace into the world around us. The only way to accomplish that is my path, to prevent that tragedy from ever occurring again; not sacrificing those we care about all over again. That's why we were promised a savior, the heir to the king of martyrs. Justice means restoring order, and I will be the one to put things back in place. From the inside, here, in the heart of the state, I—no, we—can end it here." The Supervisor held out her hand, and smiled.

Zulayka replied with her own anger, "Why should I believe any of your story? You expect me to believe that a founder of the Insurgency pulled off a complete switch and defected? And even if I fell for that, I'm supposed to not question the fact that you killed—"

The Supervisor's eyes narrowed, "Not killed. The Insurgents chose that path themselves."

"*Killed*," Zulayka finished.

"I'm doing what they wanted. At least they have the luxury of their deaths panning out in the end. I learned the hard way that not everyone gets that chance."

Zulayka plowed forward, "This doesn't add up. Do you think I was an investigator for the past 5 years for nothing?," she paused, struck by her own words. Where she was now, it had nothing to do with her investigation skills. She was the interrogator who was interrogated. Unlike the woman before her, Zulayka promised herself not to forget, not again.

Seeing her chance, the Supervisor took initiative, sensing an advantage, "Us two, Zulayka, we want the same things. Justice, the return of stability. Abraham did well in teaching you some of what you needed to know, but only I can take you to the end point. I've been watching you for a long time. I knew that the longer Isaac kept up his play revolution, more lives would be lost. I know what we need, here and now. I have spent all these years working with the same agency that took my father's and Zahra's life, because I realized it was my best chance to enact my justice and stop the Insurgency from misguiding others and condemning them. For that goal, I'll crush every insurgency in my way."

"You're insane."

"And you're not listening. I'll dip my feet in hell if it means I can raise my head towards the heavens. This path, my path is the revolution. Abraham misled you. He's exactly like his brother now—or even worse." A shadow of a smile cast itself over her face, and a sharp laugh cut through her throat, its knives of sound piercing through the floor, shocking Zulayka. "What a failure. Under Abe's watch it all fell apart. I never expected anything else. Once his execution is performed, there will be no eulogies spoken, no tears spilt, and no beauty seen."

In Zulayka's mind, the memories of Abraham flooded through her, a rushing river of droplets collapsed into a wave, united without distinction, always one with the illusion of being many. She recalled the king of hearts and his stand in the desert, the massacre of him and his family. Once, she, too, called such a performance a failure. Back then, success meant something she could see, results she could record, because that was all that mattered, because that was all that was real. But when the man who was more than a man looked to the sky that day, its blazing gold sun and cloudless blue sky, bloodied red and brown sand scorching from the heat of reflection, his trust never wavered. The eyes that saw within the blue and gold weren't his own— Abraham told her that. Through her eyes, his death, their deaths, were meaningless. But not through His eyes, the One above, the blue within the folds of the sky, the essence closer to us than the blood in our veins, the heater of the flames and igniter of the lights.

Her hurricane of thoughts settled on the earth. "You and everyone else in the upper levels, Nardeban and Bliss, what you seek is no different from what Nardeban seeks."

A dark smile gleamed from the Supervisor's face. "This again?"

"The revolution you want, it's no different from what they want for themselves. You each start and end on the same step, the same values, the same understanding. You only know how to look at, not how to see through, to see beyond. You've adopted their cynicism, and you think that you got to where you are because you're special."

For so many years, Zulayka devoted her life to peace. Peace meant foundation, constancy. It relied on her viewing the lower levelers with disdain. As hopeless and lost. "Those on the upper levels aren't higher than those here, down below. They're even more deluded, more misled, submitting to cruelty and ignorance to retain what will inevitably be lost. The dream you're reaching for is similar, isn't it? Instead of seeking more, you settle for what Nardeban wants you to settle for, and open yourself to all the same weaknesses they have. Nardeban offers you your freedom but they don't let that freedom out of its cage; they merely invite you in with it. If what Nardeban aims for is temporary and exclusionary, then so too is their motivation and resolve. We aren't alike, not anymore.

"They manipulated you, used you to destroy what you wanted to create, walking in their footsteps and kneeling when they commanded. You sold your wings for chains, thinking the earth was the sky. In a night of a thousand stars, you gazed upon the dark.

"Every step you take, every word you speak, every breath

you breathe is a debt to those martyrs whose death made them immortal and passed that same chance onto us. Conferring their knowledge and love onto us. For that alone, I will *never* join you."

The Supervisor's wood brown eyes darkened, crackling with hatred, a righteous hatred it thought, a necessary hatred. Then, it died. The icy flames subsided, curling back into their hearth with disdain. "He's gotten to you. I understand. His brother deceived me, too. Take your time, Zulayka. I will be waiting."

A cruel reflection stared back at Zulayka. A lopsided smile, eyes that teetered on the edge. A chill ran down her back, running away, bearing witness to a future before her. For a moment, doubts bubbled up to the surface. What did it mean to fail? What did it mean to succeed? Her choices led to danger. Death breathed down her neck, putting its hands on her shoulders, whispering fear and regret into her ears, envisioning the devastation of the path she could choose, following the footsteps of two dead men. What did it mean to live? And what did it mean to die? One by one, the bubbles of uncertainty popped, the wave and its foam became one with the ocean. Death was return, nothing more and nothing less. That tale from two thousand years ago, was she to accept the Supervisor telling her those deaths were pointless? The steps of sacrifice, Abraham taught her, formed the staircase of martyrdom, leading to the heavens.

"You'll be waiting for nothing. Because he has gotten to me. And because I've finally gotten to myself."

Zulayka rose and went to the door, stopping when she heard a voice call out to her.

"Once you leave here, you do realize it's over don't you? I

have a job to do, after all."

Zulayka continued outside, gas mask attached, proceeding to the Boat of Charon to rise back up and prepare. As she slowly rode up, she didn't realize it would be the last time for many years that she'd walk freely in the sky. One last task awaited her, with one day left until Abraham's execution. Nardeban might have extinguished the wildfire, but its embers remained. Zulayka raised her face to the smog of sky above her. It reached out to her, called out her name. By some otherworldly instinct, her hand rose up to greet it. It was the smoldering of an ember, the still burning lamp of Abraham deafeningly glowing in the silent darkness. She took a deep breath and remembered a moment with Abraham, during her moment of greatest doubt.

***

"Why do you waste your time on me?" Zulayka asked dejectedly. "Up until now, I spent my life in ignorance. Even now, I'm still repeating the same mistakes. I'm not someone who's worthy of this, I'm not someone who deserves this from you."

Abraham's sight narrowed with surprise. "What's wrong, Zulayka?"

"How is someone like me ever supposed to become someone like you? How can I, with my irritation and anger, match your patience? How can I, with my forgetfulness, ever match your unrelenting remembrance? How can I, with my scathing speech, manage to match your uncompromising compassion? How can I, who helped to destroy what you build, even dare to sit before you like this? I know all the overwhelming ways I need to grow now, I feel intimately and deeply those cracks in my heart. But I don't wish to be a burden to you, I don't deserve the kindness and care you've shown me. I don't deserve it. I don't deserve any of it." Bitterness and despair clothed Zulayka's words, her head bent down as her fingers dug into her knees. This guilt, this sudden roar of hopelessness was met with the soft embrace of Abraham's response.

"Dear Zulayka. Please listen to me." Hesitantly, Zulayka raised her watery gaze. "You are here for a reason. You are here because I wanted you here. You are here because God arranged for it. That awareness of your sins, that is a sign of love that you will one day be able to see. The love that carries the breath from and to your lungs, the love that channels the blood through your body, the love that colors the sight that you look out with, it is the same love that brought you closer to this point step by step, it is the same love whose mere sigh awoke you from the slumber of nonexistence. That love is the key and you are the door. You are special, everyone is special and chosen simply for being born. Oh, if only you could see the love of the hands that shaped you, the love of the light that resides within you. The brilliance waiting to shine, the perfection that has always existed, the eye of your heart blocked only by the veil of your despair. If only you could see what I could see, and all your breaths would only be spent in praise. There is no inevitability in your sins or your flaws, there is only inevitability in returning to Him. Grieve not, despair not. Faith is neither a leap nor a fall. It is flight. Do you know how much He longs for you, how much He wishes for you to gaze upon Him? Trust in the love that brought you here and trust in the love that will guide you towards infinity."

***

All were chosen the moment they were born. The Supervisor was wrong. Zulayka's eyes spilled with flowing trust, determined to save the one who flew without wings, the one who saved her.

***

I was a seed beneath a sea of leaves
Until Your light climbed down
Eyes seeing what could never be unseen
I sprouted and bloomed, fed only by the desire to meet You

This burning hope
This flaming need
It makes me more desperate
Than the world's worst greed
Ode to holy desire, from the collections of Falaq

The Twilight Horizon

The Twilight Horizon

From You, 2000 Years Ago

The hearts wept, fearing what was inevitable. The coming sun, flying beneath the earth, wrestled against itself. On this day, the sun prayed to let the night remain eternal. The stars glistened with tears, but no clouds stood by to hide them. His soldiers exited the tent solemnly, the grief of the world hanging over them, the sadness of more than a thousand years and more than a million miles. Without the martyr king, they were knights without swords, matches without flame, and a desert without oasis. The only hope that lightened their burden was the gifted knowledge that they would not live to see him die.

His sister did not have this luxury. She would bear witness to the wave of death. When something falls from one's hands, do they not try to catch it? That moment of unbreakable focus, eyes locked onto it as it slips farther and farther away, mustering every ounce of speed to propel forward, clasping blindly in front of them. The crushing defeat of opening up one's fist only to discover their palm was empty. She reached and reached, but it was as futile as keeping a wave away from the ocean, just as the dune was of the desert and the wind was of the air. His destiny marched ever closer. Its ink was as black as the night, the night they prayed would last forever.

***

Zulayka stood alone in the massive procession. It was the start of the new day, and the sky blazed awake from its cloudy dreams. Nardeban's propaganda campaign churned onwards, with today's highlight on the front page of every holographic screen: the execution of the Insurgency leaders. Once, she would have stood alongside the crowd, cheering for the end of another rebellion in a line of rebellions.

Stooped in ignorance, in forgetfulness, losing herself to the idea of victory without ever asking what was won.

The hurrahs around her seemed to quiet, their rush reduced to rain drops that she deftly dodged. Their lives moved on as normal, dreamers wandering in a daze, mistaking injustice for justice, mistaking failure for triumph. The cries for freedom fell on souls who shouted from their muzzles that they were free, as free as a bird in its gold-lined cage with a framed painting of the sky on its wall. The congregation marched onwards in religious frenzy, chanting as the preaching screens spoke of the hellfire and brimstone they avoided and the heaven and paradise that awaited them from here on out. They hollered and worshipped, convinced in the structure of the levels, their divine authority that distinguished between the chosen and the unchosen. What is freedom when it points in only one direction? What is diversity when everyone walks the same path?

Despite her own progress, Zulayka knew she wasn't ready. There was so much that eluded her, so many flaws and hidden restraints that held her back from uncovering all that lay inside her. She, who was so lost not even months before, needed to rescue the guiding hand that lifted her from these masses, away from their wails disguised as cheers. If she lost him now... Her window of opportunity was tight. There were only four hours till noon, till the scheduled execution, and only two hours till the prisoners were to be removed from their cells.

Lost in her thoughts, Zulayka walked through the parade. The upper levelers strode on giant, glowing glass platforms. A few hovercrafts zipped above them; most of the traffic was dispersed for the celebrations. More people spilled out from hover elevators, residents of Levels 2, 3, and 4, even though the march would lead them back down again. They shuffled forward frantically, diligently taking their places behind the denizens of Level 1. Zulayka skirted free, reaching a relatively undisturbed alleyway.

"Excuse me," Zulayka said, motioning to a couple blocking her way.

The husband looked back at her, annoyed. His gaze was permeated with the haughty stench of a resident from Level 1. "Who are you to order us around?" As if to ignore Zulayka's presence, the woman refused to turn back.

Gritting her teeth into a smile, Zulayka revealed her holobadge, indicating her position in the Instability Investigation branch.

Instantly, the couple's mood shifted. "I had no idea you were with the branch! I thought you were one of those lower levelers from 3 or 4. They have so much nerve since it's the only time the parade is leading us down the levels," he complained before shifting to flattery, with his wife looking on approvingly now. "Please accept my apologies and gratitude for the work you've done. Without you, none of this would have been possible. Midan has been granted a great honor. I sure hope Nardeban's been treating you right!" The two laughed together, as if they were telling a joke. But the person they were praising was no longer there.

"Ah, don't worry about it," Zulayka replied painfully. They took her brevity as humility. It was only natural for someone talking to a resident of Level 1.

As they made way for her and drifted towards the center of the moving channel, Zulayka was struck by deep shame. Her past clung to her like wet feathers. Where did their respect stem from? She limped onwards.

Zulayka weaved through the school of passersby and arrived at the prison. Checking her holophone, she tried contacting Captain Jonah one last time to gain official approval. The same error popped up, in an angry neon red.

CALLER NOT AVAILABLE.

She sighed. With a hastily forged permit in her hands, Zulayka stood at the gate and the guard motioned her through, familiar with her presence after weeks of visits. Or, at least, that was what she expected to happen.

"Hey," the guard called out to her. Zulayka slowly turned around, her heart racing. "Are you sure you're supposed to be in here? Some of these prisoners are due for their trial soon."

Trial. She almost laughed. "Yes, I've been here dozens of times, surely you recognize me by now." She strained to keep her voice nonchalant with a hint of annoyance, remaining natural.

"That was different. Today's different. I think I'm going to have to ask you to—"

Zulayka cut him off, "I'm not sure you'll want to do that. This isn't like the other times. I was sent by the Supervisor." In an almost hushed tone Zulayka said her title. It had the intended effect.

He considered his position, and responded, feigning apathy, "Whatever. Go ahead then, don't let me stop you."

Zulayka turned to the looming hallway. Time was ticking away and the crowds outside seemed to grow louder. Panic seized her mind and the elevator looked so far away and the parade's cheers taunted her every step until she broke into a jog and the officers patrolling glanced at her with suspicion and she must have pressed that accursed elevator button a hundred times by now— it finally opened. Zulayka stood motionless as she once again descended into the Void, the highest security prison in Midan. Each breath hammered against her heart, a sickly anxiety coursing through her veins. The silence of the elevator pierced her more deeply than the world's applauding of Abraham's coming death, forced to stand still as everything around her fell further down below.

The obsidian-black doors parted ways with a cruelly pleasant chime. Strobe lights hung low from the garish ceiling, flickering with a dull brightness. As she walked towards Abraham's cell, Zulayka took time to reminisce on their encounters. The fear and worry that pulsed through her pushed one memory to the forefront of her mind.

***

"Were you ever," Zulayka began hesitantly, "were you ever afraid? You were hunted for so long, and now you're caught by the same people who slaughtered and persecuted the Insurgents. Were you afraid? Are you afraid?"

"I am always afraid," Abraham replied.

"What?"

"Everyone feels fear. Our fears, our hopes, they're a reflection of our reflection, the shadow of our shadow. We can distinguish fears from one another in the same way we distinguish between right or wrong. I do not fear for my life, or my belongings, or my reputation among those who hate me. I do not fear losing these things because I do not desire them. I do not desire wealth or status or vanity. However, I am afraid. I worry for you, Zulayka, I worry for myself, I worry if my words were kind, if my actions were compassionate, if my intentions were pure. I fear anything that creates distance between Him and I. These fears are guardrails, not restraints. These fears are signs of love, of what we truly desire.

"Most people are afraid of falling. When we fall, everything is out of our power. We have no agency, no authority, and before we even hit the ground, our ego is at peril, crushed before the body. Left alone in the air, one struggles and shouts and kicks to no avail. There is no sense of control, no illusion of independence. In some ways, falling is when we are closest to the Truth. But there is one spirit that cultivates courage, one knowledge that transcends terror. When I realize that all I am belongs to Him, when all that there is, there was, there ever will be belongs to Him, then that sensation of falling, the tightening of one's chest, the sharpness of one's breath becomes calm. The ripples of the pond subside into tranquility. Losing ourselves for Him makes us weightless. My only fears are disappointing Him, disobeying Him, doubting Him.

"Are you afraid, then, dear Zulayka?" Abraham asked softly.

Zulayka looked down, and beneath the table she held her hands together. She clenched her fingers. "I am."

"Then you can decide whether your fears are chains dragging you towards the earth or wings breaking the span of an endless fall."

***

Suddenly, Zulayka was merely a few feet from the cell. He

was there. Her feet felt like they were glued into the ground by the overwhelming pressure of the miles of earth above her, threatening at any moment to break loose.

"Don't keep me waiting now," a voice called out.

Zulayka opened the cell door.

Abraham sat before her with a calm smile forming on his face, stretching into wrinkles of joy. A moppy set of black-gray hair curled up and down along his head, the same aged and loose clothes clumsily wrapped around his body.

"I came here to save you," she blurted out, the pressure of time reinvigorating itself. "There's not much time before they come to get you for the execution, we need to leave—"

"Or was it I that came here to save you?" Abraham asked, eyes twinkling.

"Sit," he motioned to the chair that was familiar with her presence. "Tell me your plan."

There's no time for this, she thought, taking a seat anyway. "We'll go up the elevator, I'll tell them there was a change of plans, that I'm the one who's supposed to be taking you to the execution, next we can—"

"What next?," Abraham replied, with a gentle sadness that burrowed deeper than wild weeping or frenzied fear. "We'll both be captured, eventually. We'll lose two lives instead of one. If you don't leave here with a founder of the Insurgency though, you'll have a chance. " No urgency bled from his voice.

Two fists formed at her side, "So, is that it?," she spat out, shielding herself under a mask of fury. "You're that willing to let everything you built go to waste? Your legacy? There are so many people who need you, but you're telling me that you aren't even willing to try? I thought you weren't afraid of that type of stuff!" Zulayka slammed her eyes shut as she shouted, tilting her face to the side. Shimmering wet stars shot down her cheek.

"Are you willing to just die here? Living is part of your mission. Your time isn't done yet. The people in Level 5 need you. Nardeban needs you. Do you expect me to accept this?" In their charge forward, her words finally presented the meaning in her heart. "How am I supposed to let you die in front of me?" Her voice broke.

Abraham cleared his throat. He felt the blessing of every breath that still flowed through him, the still warm blood that streamed in his veins, the eyes that still caught glimpses of beauty. "I will die today," he said simply. Those few words struck shame into Zulayka.

"It's a fitting topic for a final lesson, isn't it? Fitting in that death is not final and in that this lesson is not final, far from it. I have spoken to you about the heavens. What you need to understand is that death is merely the setting of the sun. And what happens at the dawn of night? All the stars are revealed under one sky. The many become one, the one and the same, the shadows tracing back the path to the light. The stars were always there, beneath the light of the sun. When you look at the night sky, what do you say? That you see nothing but infinite darkness? Or that all you can see are the endless stars? We are all from the same source, and we will all return there," Abraham continued with unshackled confidence plating every word.

Hiding the worst of her anguish, Zulayka asked, "What did

you do when Isaac died?"

Abraham sighed a sigh with layers of soft, sad memory permeating through it. "When I lost my brother, Isaac, it felt like I lost myself. He endowed me with everything he left behind, and I thought I was alone. That loneliness burned within me, left without a compass to guide me home. I lost my brother. My only family. My teacher. But in the night of grief, every tear becomes a star. And I cried every night, for all I had lost. First Zahra, then Isaac, Rabia, and soon Naamah. All stars in the sky now.

"The night is the time of contemplation, the time where our prayers travel farther, ascend higher. Our journey to Him is not unlike the stars. Search for Him in the light, in the open, and you'll find nothing. Search for His light in the darkness, and you'll find that He is everywhere. I paused and looked within, and there I found Isaac, staring back. I found myself in my sorrow. I cried because I believed I lost Isaac. The only person I lost was myself.

"You asked me about everything I helped to build. You asked me about everyone who still needs a teacher. You asked me about my legacy. The answer is staring you right in the face, Zulayka. *You* are my legacy, the one who will take the torch and blaze forward whenever its embers flicker from holder to holder. And you, like me, like the others who came before us and the ones who will come after, will realize the way through your loneliness. I taught you nothing. Everything you need already exists within you, like a marble block waiting to be carved into a sculpture. Anything you thought you learned was simply remembering what you had forgotten. Trust in Him, trust in the you that has yet to be and yet has always been. Trust until all the stars in the night become the sun."

Zulayka, with her composure slowly restoring itself, grew silent. An hour remained.

She waited. Each moment limping by, walking to its destination. Destination, destiny, and its crossroads. She broke her fast of silence and raised her gaze from the dead floor. "I owe you so much. How can I bring myself to leave this place? How can I bring myself to leave you, you who is more me than me?"

Abraham gave one last smile. "Do you know what creates sorrow? It is separation from the things and people we derive beauty from. Love, divine love, is the urge for closeness, in spirit, in reflection. And sorrow, divine sorrow, is the despair of distance."

Zulayka replied, managing a chuckle, "You must be getting old, you've told me this one before. The story about creation."

"There was one part I never got to," he said. " Once our hearts open, once we purify ourselves, we finally see the world for what it truly is. We see that His Names exist everywhere, that He is always around us. We see that separation from Him is an illusion, that all the world is love and beauty once we learn to embody His attributes and His design. The web of creation unifies, and in that recognition so do we. The clouds, the rain, the lake. The seed, the stem, the flower. The caterpillar, the cocoon, the butterfly. All are one, the one and the same. See not time, see not space. See light. See Truth. See Him. And then you will know that I am always with you, that He is always with you. Our distance is no longer defined by this world. We have transcended it.

"Do you remember the tale of the father who lost his son to the well? They were reunited, through patience. Everything that happens is His decree. I am grateful for every moment I have had with you. I am pleased with whatever He decides for me. That is my revolution. That is the path of martyrdom. Life in this cell is bitter. For us, death is like honey. Death means the death of separation."

A chime rang out as another elevator descended. "They're here early. That means it's time for you to get out of here," Abraham said. The chaos of her emotions boiled to a simmer, until they settled down altogether. Tranquility wrapped itself around her.

"Goodbye," Zulayka said with a voice intricately put back together from its shards, straining to hold together.

"Goodbye," Abraham whispered.

She walked past the guards approaching his cell, and ascended.

***

On a silver podium levitating above a massive crowd, Bliss, leader of Nardeban, appeared crowned by the sun.

"Citizens of Nardeban! Upper levelers! You who have transcended gravity! You weightless who carry the weight of this world upon your backs! We are here for the trial of our state's worst enemies. This is happening all over Nardeban, but I left the capital this morning to be with you, people of Midan!" A ravenous applause rumbled through the crowd.

"Due to the efforts of the Instability Investigation branch, the Insurgency is at its end. Before you, we have five Insurgent leaders, including two of their founders. It is time to put an end to this plague, an end to this infectious violence that has riddled the ill hearts of the abyss walkers. They incited chaos onto our levels, desiring to steal from you, to rob you of what you have earned. But they can never rob you of the qualities that make you more worthy than they will ever be! The stars bow to you, yours is the light which rivals the sun. We have dominated the night, achieving splendor after splendor. They are jealous. They can't help it.

"The Insurgency wanted to destroy what we created. They wanted to destroy you. No longer. It is time to give my verdict for this trial, on behalf of all of Nardeban: guilty!"

The sun looked on directly above the event at the center, with a ring of clouds circling the edges of the sky. Five birds stood on a lone branch, resting their feathers for the journey ahead. They were draped in shining black, chins tufted with a gleaming orange followed by a white ruffle.

Thousands gathered at the special ceremony only for the upper level residents, before them a stage. It was one of the rare times when they were brought to the bottom of Level 5, the shadows of their looming towers and opulence glaring down at them—a pointed reminder. Soldiers lined the perimeter and extended out for miles, keeping any abyss walkers at bay. The Supervisor sat to the left of Leader Bliss on their floating booth, a position of high esteem. A spectre of wrath twitched in her fingers.

Five prisoners were escorted up the raised platform and made to kneel before the crowd. Abraham, and four others. Somewhere far from here, at the edges of the clouded sky, a raindrop fell. When does a single raindrop ever fall? It is likely no one is there to see it, that no one is there to hear it. The prisoners' backs crumpled against the heat of the sun, sweat gathering at their foreheads, reflecting small rays of light on a crowd blanketed in its own shadows. On cue, they began counting down.

Five.
Four.
Three.
Two.
One.
Noon struck.
The birds flew away.

Roars trembled like a shockwave from the crowd. Shaking through each level, from One to Five. Zulayka silently exited. Head hooded, heart sheathed. A thousand stars twinkled like pearls beneath the currents of the sky, unable to be seen but burning nonetheless.

***

Just like that, not only Midan but all of Nardeban appeared to return to normalcy. Only a week has passed since the execution. The Supervisor spent that time tying up loose ends, and now all her preparations were complete. Her job was done, she could rest. She won.

A knock on her door interrupted her packing. The boxes strewn across the floor made her usually tidy office unsightly. Who would dare visit her now? She opened the door to find Zulayka.

"You again? Have you changed your mind?" The Supervisor asked, curious.

"Not at all."

The Supervisor only laughed in response. Zulayka continued, "I'm here to reject the promotion. I'm done."

The impudence to come all the way here to waste the Supervisor's time. With a snarl, she responded, "Then, you're fi—"

"I quit. All of it. The Instability Branch, the upper levels."

"Why exactly are you here? Are you foolish enough to come looking for enemies?"

"No," Zulayka smiled. The Supervisor's blood froze. "I want an ally. Someone who was trained, someone who can still choose to do what's right."

The Supervisor stared at the hand. A phantom's hand. The ghosts she chased suddenly stood before her. That smile. In that moment, she was whisked away into the land of the dead, where a buried conversation revived from its slumber.

***

"Aren't you afraid?" Rabia asked Isaac.

He smiled. It wasn't a carefree smile. It radiated some indescribable hope. It was a sad smile, and a defiant smile. Back then, that smile was a door to somewhere different. Now, she only saw it as a wall blocking her path. A young Abraham stood listening nearby, hiding. It was still an Insurgency in its infancy.

"Am I afraid? Of what, death?"

Rabia nodded.

His vision fixed itself above her head, looking past his eyes and past this sky.

"I have no reason to be."

Rabia glared at him with annoyance.

Isaac laughed, clarifying, "I didn't mean to brush your question off. What we've learned is worth a thousand lifetimes. The only thing Nardeban or anyone else can take from us is distance, reducing the distance between us and what we love. There's no hover vehicle out there that can provide faster passage than martyrdom."

Rabia fell silent.

***

Somehow, his ghost stood before her, not once but twice. How did Zulayka manage to copy him? Look through her yet within her as he once did? As his brother once did. A blistering outrage squirmed under the Supervisor's skin, that same droning desire hammering away in her mind, the restless phantom of her own that possessed her, that drove her corpse forward against the living.

Slowly, the Supervisor brought her open palm towards her, only to slap it away. Cruel, cruel laughter vibrated through her bones and jaw, eyes lighting up with darkness, memories quickly covered up like stars under the blanket of the sun.

"When you leave here, I will chase you. I see my mistake now. He's already poisoned you, like how his brother poisoned him. I will hunt you to the ends of the earth, and I'll crush your fickle justice hellbent on sacrifice. Like how I crushed each of theirs. Fear it when it comes. Fear it as it approaches. Fear it even when it's never there."

Without responding, Zulayka gazed at her with disappointment. Stunned, the Supervisor watched as Zulayka walked back out into the lonely terrain of Level 5, back onto her hovercycle, and soared away. The Supervisor looked at the closed door, knowing she should have tried to track her. But for the first time in years, her emotions overwhelmed her. This tent. It was still *that* tent. It was still *her* tent. The old woman who started all of this. The Supervisor decided then and there to have it torn down. There would be no more sentimentalism to hold her back.

She continued packing everything away until the walls were laid bare and the dark floor shimmered in reflection. The site was demolished only a few days later.

***

Zulayka came to a stop, unlatching a large bag from her bike. It appeared her last few moments of access to the Instability Investigation branch's database were worth it after all. She arrived at the Insurgency's original base. The ruins heaved before her, mercilessly run through and brought down. A warehouse razed to rubble, even after its inhabitants were long gone. A warning set in charred iron and stone. Behind its shattered frame, seemingly random strings of sunken earth stretched out from the fallen building. The Instability Investigation branch must have made sure to destroy the tunnels that let the Insurgency escape the first time.

Zulayka moved by instinct along one buried path, following it all the way to its end. At the extremities of her vision, two gray blocks sat rooted into the dirt. Gravestones. She made her way to them by foot. At this slowed pace, her eyes scanned the earth, the signs of struggle and frenzy imprinted in footsteps. Left here alone, Zulayka wondered where their owners were now.

The ants marched in their lines, shy heads of grass poking out from the sleepy soil, but they were sparse and few. It was a land on the edge of death, but it was not a dying land. Zulayka listened and watched, feeling the rhythm of the world with each step she took. Her mask suddenly felt tighter, burdensome. Motivated by nothing but a feeling, she took it off and breathed. The air was clean, as clean as one could expect for Level 5. No one had been here for a long time. The first grave was Zahra's. A small withered tree grew beside the aging stone, using its slope as a rest for its naked wooden arm. A black cloth was tied to its trunk. Zulayka slipped it off, clutching it in her hands.

The other marker, Isaac's, wasn't much farther. Despite never meeting either of them, Zulayka sensed their connection. A feeling of melancholy overcame her. She shuddered against the loneliness.

She began her work by taking out a small shovel from her bag and piercing it into the claylike ground, clearing a small rectangular space. As she took dirt out, she poured her feelings in, her final act of retribution and remembrance. This hollow breath of earth was all she needed to dig. There was no body to prepare, to read rites to, to send away with parting words. The shovel's steel mouth was sharp and silent against the gray soil. Her hands trembled, holding tightly to the handle. Only one task remained. Due to its weight, she dragged the bag alongside her up until this point, and brought out a third gravestone. The ache in her arm was numb as she planted a third gravestone beside Isaac. It read, *Abraham*. A name more familiar to her than her own. There was no item or memento to place before it, no flower or gift or a crowd to eulogize to. So she spoke silently to herself, thanking him while praising Him. She planted the seed of a promise, to realize the vision he left to her. To build a lighthouse.

The loneliness throbbed in her heart. The world to her seemed a cold and cruel place. The cheers still haunted her. The emptiness in Level 5 seemed more appropriate. All the others around her were distant from her, no matter how close she was. People she had known for years, family she spent her life with.

Abraham had spoken with her about this otherness. This soft and spiky pain. The more you know, the more you see. The more you see, the further from others you become. The state of her city hurt her heart.

"Praise be to God," Zulayka blurted out. Gratitude poured into her. Astonishing herself, a smile blossomed upon her face. Her otherness, she realized, was a blessing. The world appeared to her as a stranger, and she as a stranger to the world. She buried her last doubts into the ground, the small yearnings to abandon her duty and slip back into oblivion. But how could she? Her sleep had broken in the middle of the night and no matter how hard she tried she could not return to how she was before.

She viewed the graves before her solemnly. The memory of the king of martyrs stung her. Here she was lamenting her loneliness. His loneliness was unimaginable. New tyrants now roamed the earth. His vengeance went on unfulfilled. Injustice and corruption leaked through every crack, darkness smothered every light. Somewhere above her, Abraham flew freely now. But what about the Savior? Her mourning for Abraham became mourning for the Awaited One. Hours passed.

The brothers were reunited. Zulayka rose and stared for a

long time at the makeshift cemetery. Minutes passed, she left the shovel there and headed back to the site of destruction.

Zulayka searched through the mosaic of walls and ceilings, finding only cold ashes and shadows under the wreckage. Near what she could only assume was the entrance, however, lay a thin, tattered black scarf—once green. Something about it called out to her, speaking to Zulayka in a secret language that she heard not with her ears but with her spirit. She retrieved it, tying the solidified memory to her arm. One last time, her vision swept through the landscape. The air around her sung with a tone of finality. Her feet didn't want to leave, but the electricity of motion spurred them forward. The remaining stone in her eyes wilted away and waters of memory gushed forth, each drop revitalizing the land, awakening its forgotten heart. Compared to these tears, the rain was like sand.

***

Bird without wings
I still hear you sing
Beating that drum
So far away from
Where I am

Bird without wings
Resting in eternal spring
What must you see
Flying endlessly
To a twilight horizon

Bird without wings
Your name still rings
In our weighty hearts

That can't bear to depart
Without you

Bird without wings
What left have you to bring
When everything you have
You already gave
I see you in the air
Way, way out there
Higher than Icarus could ever dream
No wings for the sun to shine its gleam
Your memory like the image left on the eyes
After staring too long at the light
Ode to Abraham, from the collections of Falaq

Rise of the Earthshakers

Rise of the
Earthshakers

From You, 2000 Years Ago

The blood that spilt on the sands was the same as the blood that ran through his veins. One by one, he watched them leave from his makeshift bed on the ground. By fate's decree, Illness took command of his arms and legs, but its embrace was free from cruelty, its embrace was loving. It was this love which kept him from running out into the dunes. The prince of hearts looked on, heart spilling the tears that his eyes could not, robbed of even the water needed to cry.

He sat and watched as one by one his family and followers took to the battlefield. He was too weak to scream from grief. Illness hugged him tighter, begging him to stay and live, as Illness fell ill from the despair it witnessed. Every moment he prayed for the next moment, unable to console his sisters and aunts. One by one, they fell. His cousins, his brothers, his uncle. His father.

In that final moment, the moment the world was changed forever, the prince smiled. Illness gazed at him with wonder, spectator to his coronation, spectator to the praise that fought its way through his lips plagued by shivers of the skin and moistened only by the flow of its own blood. In the coming night of cries and wails, in the coming night of fire and darkness, those words were the most beautiful words that Illness ever heard. With its duty completed, Illness exited the tent, leaving the orphaned prince to his sacred sorrow.

The betrayers dragged the prince and the remnants of his family through the sands. Chained upon the back of a camel, all he saw was the figure of his grandmother watching him with care from the dunes. With the frail strength left to him, the prince raised his arm toward her, praying for Him to console her. Those fingers held the world, whispering a promise.

***

The City of Kaam was the oldest city of Nardeban. Some said Kaam was the first to institute the level system, the birthplace of verticality hundreds of years ago. Perhaps that was why it was also the site of one of the strongest Insurgent compounds. Perhaps that was why the Insurgent site at Kaam was the first to face destruction, a decade earlier than the others. Perhaps that was why the orphans left behind chose to become thieves.

"What a steal!" A lanky teen yelled, mindlessly stuffing a multicolored mess of plastics into an umbrella with a broken handle. Around him, a rally of a dozen or so kids followed suit, one shushing him with an airy hiss. Shelves surrounded them, rows and stacks of vomit-neon colored snacks. It was a corner store on Level 3 of the City of Kaam, not upscale enough for decent security but not destitute enough to hide from their greedy eyes. Floating street lights flickered a firefly gold over the polished sidewalk that led up to the corner store. The moon winked above the manmade mountains of steel and glass.

A boy with roughly cut charred black hair walked out first. Guilt kept his fingers frugal; he took only enough to sustain him and Mayar for the next few days. Mayar, a younger boy, bounded out behind him, bumping into Falaq and quickly apologizing. They put their goods beside them, settling on the strangely clean concrete. There was none of concrete's signature glint, the brief shine of a buried rock glancing against one's vision when the circumstances are just right. Instead, it was a slat of gray.

"Are we about to go back to Level 5 soon?" Mayar asked,

glancing over at Falaq with a pair of midnight eyes peeking out from his choppy brown bangs sliding down his forehead. He sounded like he already knew the answer.

Falaq nodded, bunching up his shoulders to shield from the cold and huddling closer to Mayar. "There's nothing else we really can do." Mayar pouted but understood. By now, disappointment was commonplace.

Falaq gave him a wide grin, "I'll let you eat all the chocolates this time if you want."

"Really? You better promise," Mayar beamed back.

"Of course, I promise." Falaq ruffled Mayar's hair, a quiet sign of his tenderness. Mayar leaned into him, the two brothers enjoying this little time away from Level 5. Their brotherhood was forged by care, not blood. Mayar was among the youngest of the orphans, part of the generation that had never met their parents at all. Though it wasn't like the others remembered much about their own parents even if they had lived to meet them. Falaq knew they had the upper levelers to blame for that.

Falaq fixed his vision to the sky, letting his thoughts roam across the sea of stars that so rarely appeared down below. He drifted through time, washing away into the future, and seeing nothing. What came before his life, what came after, none of these seemed to hold any weight to Falaq, floating on a shallow current. A person born in Level 5 felt the weight of all the levels above them, suffocating and crushing them. His friends knew that pressure. Because of it, they threw their years to the wind and rode alongside it, becoming as hollow as the breeze before them. A few entertained whispers of rebellion, their apathy bubbling into anger. Theirs was a fire that left no ashes, that wanted only to consume until it consumed itself. Aimless heat, scattered warmth funneled into scorching hatred. For now, though, they were all caught in limbo, left together and by themselves. Was that all there was for him too? He didn't want the life of an upper leveler—he hated them—but neither did he want this life, not for him or Mayar. When he was young, very young, he remembered things were different. When all of their parents were still alive. When Kaam hadn't struck the Insurgency. Those memories were like a taste quickly disappearing from his dust-worn tongue. He scanned the horizon, catching a rare glimpse of the sun's feathers at its edge. Then, for a flash of a second, he thought he saw someone looking back at him on the street.

But his attention was swept away.

"Snap out of it, Falaq! It's the cops!" Mayar frantically tugged at his arms, pulling him from his thoughts. Falaq knew there were never cops in Level 3 around this time, yet a haunting siren echoed down the street, a twirling ballad of blue and red harshly ribboning through the shadows. Falaq ran back in.

"Get out! NOW!" His voice, usually soft spoken, revved them into action as they charged forward. Mayar and Falaq joined the crowd, lungs ragged with fear as the sirens swung onto their street, tearing its blue-red teeth through the amber ambience.

Horror flooded Falaq's face as he turned around. Mayar dropped a case of chips and ran back for it, leaving him stranded at the tailend of their retreat, the police hovercar with its twin spotlights closing in.

"Mayar, they're right there!" It was too late.

After slowing to a stop, a man clad in a black uniform sprinkled with insignia exited the hovercar. Something was off about him. Mayar's nose twitched. The officer's stench was sickly and acrid, his walk disjointed and fractured. The police hovercar, usually dangerously sheen, was clearly damaged, with its windows shattered and scattered bullet holes on its sides. Mayar felt fear override his nerves, staring as the figure approached him, a center of black in the midst of a blue and red.

"How did a little mole wander his way all the way up here?" The cop asked, with whimsical cruelty. His uniform didn't fit him, oversized and bulky compared to the thinning body underneath. Mayar kept his jaw rigid as stone. Both of them glanced at Falaq as his run fizzled into a cautious series of steps that reverberated sound on the alarmingly hollow seeming pavement. Turn back, his steps said, as ice thawed on his back, as roots of terror plunged into the ground around him. Falaq faltered, he blinked, a piercing shot of hesitation and doubt forcing him to grit his teeth. What saved his heart was a brief memory. A father's mute lips telling him a lesson. The words were lost to him but he remembered the meaning it struggled to contain as a faint tickle of smoke breathed in his nose. It exploded into an inferno of conviction, burning away the ice and the roots, propelling him closer to Mayar.

The officer did a sweep of the area, then directed his attention back to the kids, satisfied. "Good. No one's here. Looks like I can have some fun tonight while I'm waiting for my real objective," he announced with a grin, every movement unnatural. Intoxication. "Moles are basically rodents aren't they? Answer me, you, the taller one."

Despite the panic, Falaq responded normally, as if his words might alter the reality before them. "Yeah, I think so. I don't really know." Inside, he seethed. The man seemed to flirt with the gun on his holster.

"And rodents ought to be exterminated." His hand finally fell to the gun. "Tell me, do you know what this is? Have you seen one before?" He pulled out the gun. It was a sleek, vantablack firearm. It absorbed the very night around it.

"These are called Shade-eaters. Wanna know why?" Falaq didn't answer, his attention trained on the gun's barrel. There was no way to put any bullets into it. The officer went on anyway, "It's because it shoots solid darkness, at the speed of dark. Think of how fast a shadow falls, how fast it drapes over the ground. Nothing is quicker than this."

"What about light?" Mayar blurted out.

"As if anyone could make something that could shoot at the speed of light. Besides, it's *faster*," the cop chuckled, focusing instead now on Falaq.

"You, boy, you'll get to live. So you can tell your friends back there *all* about what's about to happen." To him, this was all reasonable. Fair. Understandable. "Aren't you lucky?" He shifted his gaze, now filled with laughing malice, towards Mayar. "And aren't you not?" An aura of restlessness permeated from him, tinged in madness.

Falaq shook with fury. "You upper levelers are insane. Haven't you ruined our lives enough? Is it not enough that you killed our parents?"

The cop's eyes widened, "That's right. This is Kaam, isn't it?" Wait, Falaq thought, this cop wasn't from Kaam? "You're the criminal orphans the Insurgency abandoned. I wouldn't blame Nardeban for that." Without warning, the cop suddenly shot a floating street light. "Oops."

"Wait!" Falaq yelled, trying to buy time. "Why wouldn't you capture me, or the rest of us? Can't we return the goods?"

The man clicked his tongue three times, scolding Falaq. "I don't care that you stole anything." Falaq stared back. "What matters is that you thought you could."

Sensing incoming danger, Falaq's legs sprung into action, leaping forward in front of the shot as he shouted for Mayar to run away while he still could. Time's flow tapered out, and anguish seized his heart. The vantablack head was raised and he watched the officer's finger stretch through that tiny pocket of air and recoil towards the trigger. Falaq closed his eyes, accepting that it was his time to die. He opened them, still alive on the ground with a few bruises. His own breath shocked him. The officer clutched his empty hand, the gun shot out into the sides untouched by the floating street lamps.

"Who's there?" the man shouted in fear towards the alleyway beside him, retrieving a regulation blade from his belt. It was completely rectangular and two feet long, reflecting a pale gray.

A woman burst free from the darkness, taking advantage of the cop's drunken and surprised state. In one swift motion, the blade switched hands and her fist rooted into the cop's jaw, rocking his skull into sleep.

Falaq and Mayar picked themselves up, with the latter finally speaking. "Thank you for saving us! Miss…"

Falaq noticed a black band tied on her arm as the stranger turned around and smiled. "I'm Zulayka. You two better come with me before anyone else shows up." Stunned, the two merely nodded and followed her down back into Level 5.

***

It had been a year since Zulayka left Midan. Since her departure, she kept quiet, becoming a vagabond from city to city and witnessing the same ills again and again. Along the way, she gathered remnants waiting for her at old Insurgent compounds, peeking out from the rubble, charred with permanent shadows. An invisible hand guided her to Kaam, to these two. She sensed potential in them. Especially the older one, Falaq. He jumped in front of the younger boy to save his life. After feeding them a proper meal, she provided them with a tent, where they were sound asleep. Zulayka rested by the hastily made fire, unfurling the notes she discovered during her last trip.

Meanwhile, inside the tent, Falaq remained awake. Mayar snored softly beside him with a full stomach and lightened heart. Mayar, like anyone else from these wastelands, like Falaq himself, was always guarded towards strangers. No one treated abyss walkers like humans, especially after knowing they were the children of previous Insurgents. Despite this, Mayar got along well with Zulayka. Though hesitant to admit it, Falaq liked her too. There was some sincerity that marked her, a shining glint in otherwise barren gravel. He flipped to his side, resting back into the green cover. Earlier, Zulayka inquired about their lives, and Falaq found himself responding as if she was someone he'd known for years. There was security in her presence, a benevolence he couldn't quite place. One question of hers in particular, however, threw him off.

"What do you know about the Insurgency?"

Kaam was a city where its branch of the Insurgency was wiped out in its infancy. It happened before Mayar learned how to walk, before Falaq turned six years old. His parents, and the parents of the others they knew were killed for their membership in a slaughter by the forces of Nardeban. Leaving the Orphans of Kaam to fend for themselves. Kaam held a tight watch on them for years, branding itself the most Insurgency-free city in all of Nardeban. After the fall of the Insurgency across Nardeban, they loosened up. There wasn't any real threat to crack down on, and spirits were already broken. During their lockdown, any information on the Insurgency was tightly suppressed. Kaam told the orphans that their parents were killers and murderers. None of the orphans truly knew what exactly their parents fought for. Most didn't care. Those who did usually left Kaam. They weren't seen again.

Zulayka knew the truth of that day, the day a decade ago when all the Insurgents were wiped out in Kaam. She was raised to believe the Insurgency was responsible for horrifying killings in the upper levels, but documents in the Instability Investigation branch revealed those reports were all fabricated. The total decimation of this base was meant to serve as a warning to Insurgent bases everywhere. It didn't work.

So, she offered to teach him about the Insurgency. He accepted.

"Looks like we might stick around here for a bit, Mayar." Of course, Mayar didn't respond, still deep in sleep.

Outside, Zulayka continued to read the journal she uncovered. Abraham's journal.

Entry 1- I still feel the weight of his loss, though I know he remains. What must he think of me? Already, some are deserting, their shock of losing Isaac and their uncertainty of me pushing them away. Writing through it, I hope, will bring me clarity. As long as I trust in the One above. Rousing from my misery, I found myself trapped within the spell of impatience, my tongue sharp and tempered. I lashed out in arrogance. Anyone's suggestions loomed like orders to me. He left his holy project for me to continue, and this pride flamed inside my words. I sped up plans and pushed deadlines, coldly and mechanically. Pride and grief. My heart grew distant, its connection to the light disrupted, though not ruptured. I sensed my own distance, and the light of my ambition ignited memories of her… Rabia. I've shoved away her disappearance in the back of mind ever since that day, the words she said to him. The things she's doing now, it makes me almost glad that Isaac isn't here to see it. I don't know where she is now, but I know where I want to be. Remembering her, remembering Isaac, it struck me back into place. Not once did I see him prideful. Not once did he rush, not when he knew the costs. Not once was his heart beholden to senseless sorrow. To whoever finds themselves reading this, to anyone who struggles carrying on this banner, know this. The legs that push you forward, the eyes that illuminate the path ahead, the hands that forge the future are not your own. The more you begin to know, the more you know that you've only begun. There are few idols as powerful as the idol of the self. Break it, and be free. Fail to do so, and you drag those you try to uplift down with you.

Signed, Abraham

***

"Wake up, wake up, wake up!" Mayar bellowed, tackling Falaq out of his dreams. "Miss Zulayka's calling us."

Falaq scrambled himself together, and joined Mayar and Zulayka on a walk away from their campsite.

"A change of scenery wouldn't hurt," she said.

They made their way to a small but pulsing tributary, hairs of green crowding its sides. The sound of moving water relaxed Falaq. There was life around him; surely that meant something.

Falaq turned to her. "Why are we here for the lesson?"

"You'll see."

Falaq accepted that answer, keenly listening to the water's chatter. He once again embarked on the ship of his thoughts. Mayar played in the stream, splashing it and staring at it with wide-eyed surprise. It was the rare time of the morning where the sun shone through the wall of smog onto Level 5. It was the time of morning when one's senses were blurry, grasping the light touching their face and the wobbly feeling of their legs and the weak grips of their hands. Like the world was loading before you, being re-made. Mayar chased dragon flies down the stream, astounded by their loud colors. Falaq chased his own dragon flies, the daydream only broken by Zulayka's voice.

"Let's start."

Mayar hurried back while Falaq snapped back into reality, asking, "So what can you teach us about the Insurgency? About what our parents fought for?"

The air seemed to grow still as Zulayka spoke. "They fought for revolution. Do you know what that means?"
Mayar answered. "That's when people want to overthrow the government, I think. So they can make a new one?"

"That is a definition of revolution," Zulayka affirmed, "but that wasn't what the Insurgency sought. It does touch on one important idea though, the fact that all revolutions require a process of destruction and creation. Something must be destroyed, then something must be created."

"So, what were they trying to get rid of?" Falaq questioned. Mayar pursed his lips in curiosity.

"That's a great question," Zulayka looked at him fondly. "The answer is themselves," Zulayka replied. In response to their dual looks of confusion, she continued, "The revolution your parents waged, that people across the state waged, it was a revolution within their hearts. A quest to root out the bad and plant the good, and to use their inner light to combat external darkness. To them, that was what it meant to destroy the state, by breaking through the lies the state taught them about themselves."

"Which lies?" Falaq inquired, voice twinged with a hint of annoyance. Something made him feel defensive.

"The lies that make Nardeban powerful. Nardeban isn't powerful because it controls an army or because it controls wealth. It's powerful because it controls how we think. Our very desires. You've seen it in those around you, haven't you? Whether it's someone in the upper levels or someone all the way down in Level 5, they want and reach for the same things. It is never about toppling the levels; it's only about reaching the top so that someone else can't. Their dreams are a reflection of who they are, of what controls them, of what they've sold themselves to. The oppressed seek the same strengths as their oppressor, and it is for that reason that oppression can continue. After all, fire can't fight fire. You can see the same thing happen to past rebellions, before the Insurgency. They never took time to build themselves up, and they desired as their conqueror's desired and acted as their conqueror's acted and thought as their conqueror's thought. For anyone, no matter which level they're on, the way to view Nardeban or ourselves should never be how Nardeban views itself or how Nardeban views us. Nardeban views themselves as strong because of their wealth, their technology. But is that strength? They view us as weak because of our resistance to them, our whole identity in their eyes is defined by the existence of Nardeban. But is that weakness? Is that how rebels should allow themselves to be defined, in relation to what they're trying to replace? Those rebels neither destroyed nor created; they didn't abandon an old path or try to carve a new one. They were different only in name and shell, not in substance."

Mayar chimed in, "Then what made the Insurgency different from the rest of the rebellions?"

Falaq's thoughts churned. He started wondering about Zulayka, where exactly she came from.

"The Insurgency is a lighthouse that guides people back to their source, their home, their return. The Insurgency encourages people to ascend, to ascend not through the levels but through themselves. To first strike against the enemies within their own hearts, and then to open themselves to the worlds beyond the physical and material that existed within themselves. The Insurgency never defined itself through Nardeban, it defined Nardeban through itself. Nardeban was no longer treated as the truth. This world as they portrayed it was no longer seen as the truth. The truth was what remained inside. So if you want to learn more about your parents, to learn more about the Insurgency, then you'll need to learn more about yourselves. Everything you need is already within you."

Falaq shook his head, frustrated.

"What's wrong?" Zulayka asked.

"None of this has anything to do with our parents. Nothing to do with why they all got caught and left us. It has nothing to do with why they died," his words gathered force as they marched, each one taller and fiercer than the last. "And you, you're an upper leveler aren't you?" He accused, suspicion filling his voice. That was all his mind could think about. "That would explain how you have all this stuff, like that hovercycle, like how you knew how to fight like that. I don't know what you want from us two, but I think it's better if you leave us alone." Falaq turned to his brother. "We can't trust her, Mayar." Falaq tugged on Mayar's shoulder.

"But… she seems nice, Falaq. Does it really matter that she's an upper leveler? Besides if we want to know why they died, shouldn't we learn about how they lived?" Mayar asked, shining with sincerity. "The Insurgency was different from other rebellions. Maybe she's different from other upper levelers." Falaq recoiled from his own cynicism, his young friend's words grazing his heart. He steered his thoughts back on course, a lighthouse finally in range. Zulayka watched the two carefully, compassion glimmering in her gaze.

"Do you know what it means to be willing to die for something?" she asked softly.

Falaq's face filled with shock.

His bitterness that resided within him, his bitterness against Kaam and the Insurgency that took his parents away, his bitterness against anyone complicit, he felt it pulse inside him. Zulayka saved them. She was going out of her way to reach out to them. Her kindness towards him, his realization of it made him ashamed of his outburst. His iron fingers loosened and let his bitterness fall into the sea. His disdain for upper levelers would take its time to sink, but he opened up his vision to see beyond the world as he knew it, to try and see it as his parents saw it, as Zulayka saw it. Something about it called out to him, knocking on the door to his heart. He wanted to see who was on the other side. "I'm sorry," Falaq started.

"Why don't we head back for now?" she suggested gently, and the three traveled back to her campsite. On their trek back, Zulayka recalled Abraham's notes, drawing from the comfort of his presence. Her fingers flexed at the faint sunlight landing upon them.

Entry 2- Up until now, I have spent my journey purely as a student. With Isaac's passing, the mantle of leadership left to me includes my responsibility as a guide, as a teacher, so that our struggle rises into a struggle within. In my brother's research, there was a term he discovered for it, long forgotten over the centuries—the Greater War. Thus, our outward battle against the state became our second step, against external manifestations of injustice and inequality. Our greater aim was the elimination of injustice from within oneself, mastering one's desires, overcoming our limitations and weaknesses in order to evolve into something greater. Without that internal strength, our dreams of societal justice are far off. That discipline flows through me, and Isaac trusted me to continue his instruction. At first, my impatience drove me. Then, I remembered how he taught, choosing gentleness over firmness, and through his touch he transfigured, like the alchemists of old. Alchemists turned coal into gold, revealing the gold that was always there but never seen by the untrained eye. Isaac turned education into love, through the lens which is not merely seen through, through the lens which transforms whatever it gazes upon. Finally I recognized my goal. Where I fruitlessly strived to create something new, I merely needed to draw out the light that was already there. Speak from the heart, and you will speak to hearts. For the inward journey is always the journey of return.

Signed, Abraham

***

As they neared the tents, Zulayka spied an opportunity to speak again.

"The Insurgency's goal didn't pop out of nowhere," she said. Falaq and Mayar glanced back at her.

"It all started with a story, the tragedy of—" Zulayka paused as her eyes widened when they arrived.

The Orphans of Kaam flooded the site, looting every last corner. A few started wonderingly at the hovercycle, clueless on how it managed to float before them. They tied it down with some rocks out of curiosity, seeing how much weight it might take for it to finally touch the ground. It only took a few moments for the kids to realize their latest operation had been intruded on.

"Hey now, you three better get out— wait a second! Everyone, it's Falaq and Mayar!" One shouted, and the rest tackled the two with a simultaneously painful and gratifying amount of hugs and tears.

Falaq was shocked. "It never even occurred to me that you all thought we were…"

"We thought you were dead!" one girl yelled. Solemn looks spread across the group.

"Who's that lady with you?"

Before Zulayka could open her mouth, Mayar proudly introduced her, "This is Miss Zulayka, she saved us!"

The orphans were stunned. The idea of someone putting their own life on the line to save one of them endeared Zulayka to them instantly. Few ever intervened on their behalf.

"How did you do it? How did you all manage to get away from that cop?"asked a boy, who was around the same age as Falaq.

Falaq and Mayar narrated the whole incident to the other orphans, their eyes widening in sympathy and awe.

"She took him out in one punch!"

"Does that mean she was faster than even that Shade-eater?"

"Falaq, you were so brave!"

Their voices multiplied together, with a growing admiration for Zulayka. She had earned their respect. Her manner, too, put them off. The other adults still remaining in Level 5 completely avoided the Orphans of Kaam, terrified of any association to kids related to the Insurgency. They were brushed aside, ignored, without anyone to emulate, without anything to guide them. They wandered aimlessly, some vengeful, some apathetic, some in between. For the Orphans of Kaam, Zulayka was finally something, someone, new.

"Where did you even learn how to fight like that, Zulayka?" one asked.

"And can you teach us?" another added.

Zulayka's combat ability was from her time at the Instability Investigation branch. Starting out as an agent, they trained to neutralize enemy rebels, techniques designed to outmatch any guerilla fighter. It was what she needed to rise through the ranks of the branch. Zulayka was glad those skills finally came into use for the right side. But she couldn't tell them where she learned to fight; if they all knew she was an upper leveler, they might not be as understanding as Falaq.

Falaq noticed Zulayka's pause. He stepped in. "Don't waste your time asking about any of that type of stuff," Falaq suddenly spoke out. Mayar and the rest of the orphans turned to him. "She can tell you about the Insurgency."

Just its name inspired a thoughtful, conflicted silence.

"Would you all like to learn more about the Insurgency? About what your parents fought for?" Zulayka asked, words laced with care.

Their curiosity, the inner yearning of their hearts, spoke for them. Zulayka smiled.

Entry 3- At the end of my lessons, I always make it a point to remind my students that they have, as of yet, learned nothing. The first timers are confused: how can a teacher say that? Knowledge is not merely the root or the trunk or the branch or the leaves or the fruit; knowledge is the tree itself. Our abstract discussions, our spiritual dialogues, these are only one component of what it means to be revolutionary. They will only have truly learned when their knowledge is not distinct from them, when what they know is neither what they say nor what they do; they will have learned when what they know is who they are, the very fabric of their being, the essence of everything they think and see and do. Learning is not a memorized fact or perfunctory act, it must be embraced by the heart of the student. I struggled with this at first, struggled with attaining a knowledge that was attaining me. In order to break down the falsehoods instilled in me, I needed to recognize the cracks in my foundation, to penetrate into the source of all I know, the underlying assumptions that I take as natural as my own breath. If my students, my Revolutionaries, fail to understand this point, then I taught them nothing. How does one conquer the self? By becoming something else entirely, someone they aren't, yet always were and always will be.

Signed, Abraham

***

By the end of the first day, a few orphans had already left.

"The vision of the Insurgency, the one your parents rallied behind, was not rooted in this world. It was rooted, as all things are rooted, in God," Zulayka said.

The first faction to leave were the oldest of the group.

"So they were fanatics?" an older orphan questioned harshly. "I've been around these dumps for long enough to know nothing and no one has helped me. We've been alone our whole lives." An arrogance flamed beneath them, the arrogance of a son of Adam.

"You are never alone, none of you ever were," Zulayka said.

"Then where do we see Him? Where is He? Why can't I see or hear Him?" his voice was strained, pained.

"He is to your right, and He is to your left. He is in front of you, and He is behind you. And He is always above you, and He is always watching keenly. You do not see Him, but He

103

sees You, He is the green of the plants and the blue of the waters and the yellow of the sands. He is the world around you, He is the world within you. He is the sun, but you are the cloud. You are angry. You are distraught. If you, and those who agree with you, leave now, then at least let me leave you with these words. In every moment you felt you were alone, He was there beside you. For every cry you let out in the dark, He was listening to you. He is the light that shines off of every tear. It was His love that drove Him to create you, His love that hopes you will find Him."

"Why were our parents taken from us, why were we shunned?" Another spoke out, confused and uncertain.

"Your parents fell as martyrs. Their love for Him reflected in their love for you. The challenges you have faced, these are all signs of His love, His beckoning toward you. It is your test, your test to rise and answer Him. Come with me and I can teach you how to answer Him."

Some walked away. Their doubts and their loneliness were too strong for them to overcome. Others, whose blinking eyes wrestled against the laurels of sleep, stayed. Despite what they had gone through, perhaps because of it, they stayed in order to learn why they suffered what they suffered and how to become different. They no longer sought change in the wastelands.

After the eldest, the next to leave were the vengeful.

"What do you mean their revolution was about what's inside? What's inside aint what's gonna put food in my stomach! What's inside didn't help our parents and it didn't help us either," one said.

"What is it you want?" Zulayka asked.

"I want a better home, I want to not have to live every day worrying about how I'll make it to the next. I want things to be fair, I want the things the upper levelers have, the things they take from us. I want *justice*."

"We all want those things," Zulayka said, "In the future your parents sought, it was never that those material gains didn't matter. But attaining those in it of itself is not justice. They didn't confuse the means for the ends. When an Insurgent wanted to rise, it was never about merely rising through the levels or bringing them down to the earth. Rising meant to entirely transcend those, to envision something else, to imagine something better. By all means, you should organize, you should plan, you should fight, once you know what you should be fighting for. But you need to be ready. You need to prepare before you can act."

"You're acting like we have all this time," a dejected boy cried out, his hair in a tight black bun.

"Whether or not you have time, you still need patience, time to reflect on the important questions."

"Important questions?" A spark hummed in some of their eyes. Beyond the skeptics and would-be rebels of the orphans, there were those who had long since fallen into oblivion. Some considered their life idyllic. They roamed the wastelands, formed a close band with the others, and raided the upper levels when they needed to. It wasn't glamorous. A gang of marauders, stalking the emptiness below. As they accepted the abyss, the abyss accepted them. Little did they know, their lives, fueled by the latest pleasure, ignited by the newest desire, weren't all that different from the lives of those on the upper levels. Through living in the moment, they forget their past and their future, bereft even of the present. Those who didn't look towards the horizon, those who became their own shadow, they had no need to reflect.

"Questions about who you are, where you came from, where you're meant to go. If you're unable to answer those, then what does anything else mean? If you're walking, you must be walking somewhere, but can you even tell? Have you thought about it, or are you moving forward with a blindfold?"

These discussions went on long into the night. Once dawn arrived, only a few of the orphans decided to remain.

A week passed, with the orphans lingering at Zulayka's camp. They were a rough and tumble group. They jeered and insulted before they thought, they were selfish and covetous of what little they had. But they listened to her stories, collecting the dust of her words to accumulate into pearls. The tales of Karbala, the loyalty of Abbas, the steadfastness of Zuljinah, the nobility of Zainab, the loneliness of Hussein. When the orphans looked into the vestiges of these martyrs, the puddles of their blood and sacrifice left on the earth, they did not always see themselves. When the orphans looked into the twisted shadows of the enemy, the darkness of Yazid, they began to question their own reflections.

Hands abundant with scarcity uncoiled into generosity. Tongues sharp as whips melted into ribbons of care. At times, their temptations stole their resolve from under their feet, and they found themselves stumbling back down. But their hearts were stirring awake from a forgetful sleep and their memories propelled them back on their feet. It was their first step in the right direction, a wink of light in a cave. Those who are faithful, however, are tested.

***

Their meetings would be short lived. One night, distracted by their own conversation, the Orphans of Kaam and Zulayka failed to notice the black-clad officer in an oversized uniform limping behind the tent, ears flaming when he heard Zulayka's name. He moved like a shadow, listening and waiting for a chance to strike.

"Hey, Falaq, what are you writing?" Ishmael asked, peering down at Falaq's makeshift desk.

He restrained his hand from hiding his words on instinct. He lingered by Zulayka's tent, unaware he was only a few feet away from someone who had nearly killed him.

"I was writing a poem," Falaq said nonchalantly.

"What about?" Ish pressed, oblivious. Zulayka roamed near, to Falaq's horror.

"It's a short poem. About some of the stories Zulayka told us."

Zulayka finally closed in, "Oh really? If you're comfortable, could I read it?" Ish nodded vigorously. Few of the orphans knew Falaq wrote at all. Mayar and Ish were some of the only exceptions. The officer's breath quickened. He knew exactly what stories Zulayka was telling.

She moved back close to the tent, and he seized his opportunity. He crept forward, gun in hand. With a sudden jerk, he reached out and grabbed her, aiming his vantablack firearm towards her head. Ish and Falaq froze up, with the others unaware of the intruder.

"Well, well, well. I didn't think I'd see you here again. It must be my lucky day," the man sneered, pressing the cylinder down tighter. Falaq looked on in horror. His cold words sent a shockwave through the Orphans of Kaam as they turned to the scene.

But Zulayka recognized him from somewhere else. His voice rasped a familiar tune, his face still glimmered in recognition beneath its new scars. It was Captain Jonah, her higher up during her time at the Instability Investigation branch. Here was her past, revived with a thirst for death. His head barely clung onto bare threads of black hair, wrinkles running through his forehead like valleys, and eyes poisoned with some sort of red-lined mania dancing at their edges— traces of faded intoxication. An out of place stitch covered a part of his neck, marked by a festering purple.

"What are you doing here, Jonah?" Zulayka asked, scanning for any way to break through his headlock. But any move she made could endanger the orphans. She needed to play along and stall him. She settled her thumping heart, taking a breath.

He disregarded her, vision glued on the crowd before him. "Trust me, none of you want anything to do with her." Rebels, he learned from the Supervisor long ago, were fickle. Old prejudices always overpowered solidarity. He would give Zulayka a rude awakening. "She's an investigator from the upper levels, working with Nardeban. She's spent her whole life working against you," the ex-Captain Jonah taunted, noting the immediate suspicion raining down on the kids' clouded faces. Only Falaq and Mayar's faces shone through. Retrieving a pair of vantablack cuffs from his pocket, Jonah secured Zulayka as the cuffs zapped shut with a beam of solid dark tying them together.

"I have no business with the rest of you," he said, looking directly at Falaq and Mayar.

Mayar opened his mouth to speak, but Falaq held him back.

Jonah wondered at their looks of worry on Zulayka's behalf. "This woman is a lunatic," he stressed, "Continue your lives as before." His own convincing made him uneasy. Something like this wasn't to be taken seriously. Like all the others, they would give up.

With those few words, he walked forward and took the hovercycle. Something about the two unnerved him. Abyss walkers were never supposed to look defiant. How was Zulayka able to change them so quickly? Jonah tightened the vantablack cuffs on Zulayka in his own frustration, hoping to restrain his own lurking misgivings. He wanted to get out of Kaam's Level 5 as soon as possible.

The others backed off, some with gazes shifted towards the earth or the sky. Turning back one last time, Zulayka slowly shook her head at Falaq and Mayar.

An odd sound grazed across the rough soil as they sped away. Falaq gripped Mayar's shoulder gently as they both looked on helplessly to the kicked up clouds of sand.

Entry 4- What do I seek from my students? What do I seek from Revolutionaries? After having guided them for so long now, neglecting this very journal during that time, I find myself preoccupied with these questions. I reflect on our shared trials and tests and recall what I felt in our moments of deepest danger, when our project threatened to fall apart. I witnessed them overcome their desires and limits, emerge from their cocoons, and become the people I rely upon. It was a strange sensation at first, the swelling of camaraderie, the sense of discovering fellow wayfarers on the path who had just discovered themselves. I watched their first true awakening, looking as their hearts blinked against the ocean of light before them. Selflessness and sacrifice, the willingness to put their lives, their material existence on the line, for the sake of preserving the mission of the king of martyrs.

Signed, Abraham

***

The gliding wheels spun to a stop before a wreck of a building on Level 4 of Kaam. Ex-Captain Jonah brought Zulayka inside, seating her near a wall that seemed almost too tired to stand. The ceiling heaved dangerously, like eyebags at the end of a long day, the lights winked with drowsiness, the whole complex creaked with an ache for sleep.

"Since we don't appear to be doing much else, you might as well entertain my questions," Zulayka remarked, answered by a grunt as Jonah busied himself with a holophone.

"Old habits die hard, huh?" Jonah said with disinterest.

"Don't worry, I'll start with an easy one. What are you doing here?"

His mood instantly darkened with displeasure, his still inflamed scar twitching and writhing beneath his chin. "It was her. It was the Supervisor. I didn't do anything except for what I was told. I listened to those recordings, I passed them on, I served as her liaison to the Midan department for the Instability Investigation branch." Jonah directed his glare towards Zulayka. "Once you left, she went ballistic. You're the one that got away, and she lets *no one* get away. I had already been detained, but they were supposed to let me go. But the Supervisor decided that exposure to those recordings was enough reason to cut me loose. Permanently. She wanted you, but you were long gone. And I was the one who paid the price for it."

Zulayka slipped into contemplation as the Supervisor's cruelty dawned on her. Zulayka felt his fury dripping in every word he spoke, but it wasn't just directed at her. She became keenly aware of the black scarf bound to her arm, a woven memory of times past. "I'm sorry that she went after you, Jonah. But that doesn't explain how you ended up in Kaam. What do you hope to get out of capturing me?"

While fiddling with his holophone, Jonah responded, "I have a friend here in the Kaam police force. It took me a while to get here as I recovered and hid. I'm sure they all thought I was dead. But these sad days are about to come to an end." A sinking frown carved its way on his mouth. "It's not like I wanted to do any of this. I have to. If I give the Supervisor what she wants, if I can give her *you*, then I can prove myself. Or if she comes here herself, my revenge can come quickly. It's only a matter of time, I already sent the message."

Zulayka let out a laugh, lying back against the wall.

Her laughter incited no fury from him. Jonah was tired. His malice was reserved for the Supervisor. The leftover madness dispersed. "You have no reason to be laughing. That movement you were trying to start over here with those kids and the others across Nardeban will be nothing but a dream. The Insurgency is dead. I thought you were pragmatic, Zulayka. You chose this path, following that rebel leader to his grave. Now you're trying to fool some orphans to fight a battle their parents already lost? I'm doing them a favor. No one saved me, and no one will be able to save you."

"Sorry to burst your bubble. Those kids are going to come save me," Zulayka declared.

The ex-captain was intrigued. "You really think those abyss walkers are going to come after you? These people down here don't have a shred of decency to them. They have no allegiances. They abandoned the Insurgency when times got tough. I remember the attacks on the Insurgent compounds in Midan. All it took was a few stray shots and loose threats to break most of their wills, they spilled out like fish in a barrel. These orphans barely know you, and now they know you're an upper leveler. Give your fantasies a rest. No one is good enough to change in a week, not even after years. Isn't the Insurgency's failure proof of that?"

Zulayka replied smoothly, "How could the Insurgency have failed when I'm right here in front of you? I changed, and that's the exact reason they need you to capture me."

Jonah averted his view, silent.

"You'll see, Jonah. Sometimes you just need to have faith."

***

"There's no way we're going after her," a lanky brown-haired girl declared. Much of the camp grumbled in agreement. Their distrust roared alongside the bonfire of scraps, converting rubbish into light. Destruction into creation. Falaq watched the fire quietly.

"We have to," Mayar said quietly. Then, louder, "We have to. We have to save her."

One indignant boy responded, "We don't owe her anything Mayar!"

Mayar turned towards Falaq and met his eyes. Falaq glowed with resolution. "Mayar's right," Falaq announced. "She put her life on the line to stop that cop. It's our fault that she's there in the first place."

"But she's an upper leveler!" A voice reminded from the swaying shadows.

"You're gonna believe that because the cop who tried to kill us said it?" Ignoring the fact he knew it was true, Falaq went on, "Even if she is, that doesn't change anything. She knows about the Insurgency. There's more we can learn from her. Not just about how to fight back, but about how to fight for ourselves. In the same way our parents did."

He gritted his teeth as he saw more and more of them start to move away. The bonfire swelled for a moment, and he felt his words burn his way through him. Falaq opened his mouth but only smoke came out. The revolution against himself, against all his flaws, was still unfinished. He hadn't been cooked all the way through. Instead, he stammered, "They would have wanted us to grow, to become better people. I know that I don't know how to do that by myself. Up until now, every day has felt the same as the last. After this whole week with her, how can you not feel it? When it comes down to it, you were all going to run away like the others, is that it? At the very least, aren't you curious?" "Look, Falaq, we get what you're saying. But none of that explains why we should be risking our lives. We got lucky today, that lunatic seemed lenient. Let's stick with whatever we have, whatever hasn't been stolen," said another orphan as he walked away.

"We've already let Nardeban take away so much from us, so will all of you let them take away our only chance to know our past? Will you let them take her?" From behind, Mayar grabbed Falaq's hand and flashed a smile that lit up the night. All it takes is a flint to ignite the spark of divinity. When the ash was blown away, a few embers still smoldered. The Orphans of Kaam, those who remained with Falaq and Mayar, began their preparations.

"But how are we going to find them?" Mayar realized. Falaq's face fell. The thought didn't cross his mind.

Abashedly, one teen stepped forward. "Well, uh, before you guys got here we were sort of messing with her hovercraft. Long story short, we tied a couple of rocks on the end of it. There might be a trail left." Somewhere far up above them, past the levels and highest skyscrapers, the dawning moon glew its golden grin.

***

There is no time more sacred than the night. It is when one is alone, it is when one is most vulnerable. Shrouded in black, the brightest lights shine even brighter. It is when one is closest to Him, tearing through the world of veils. Zulayka knew this as she sat, hands bound yet unshackled. With or without the sun, her eyes saw the stars.

The hours of silence drilled away at the ex-captain, her words still revolving in his head. To him, the night was the sickly poison of awareness, the blinding light's glare against his eyelids. The night brought out the differences between people.

A knock interrupted Jonah's wanderings. He rose and opened the door, peering out into the polluted wastelands. Cold beads of sweat formed at the back of his neck. Carefully, Jonah stepped outside, one hand resting on his holster, the Shade-eater, the other pushing the door back. Until the door came to a rough stop, something or someone standing between the door and the wall. *Idiots, did they think they could really hide behind the door?* Jonah whipped forward and aimed at… the broken branches. By the time he saw through their plan it was too late. The six of them pounced on him from behind, knocking the gun out of his hand.

"There's no way…" he muttered, face pressed against the dirt.

In the building, Zulayka smiled.

"You three hold him down while Ish ties him up," Falaq said, receiving a chorus of nods in response. He went inside with Mayar, holding the chip to the vantablack cuffs. "Looks like we're even," Zulayka said joyously.

Falaq shook his head. "Nah, not yet. Not until you're actually out of here." Mayar nodded affirmatively.

Their reunion was cut short as the others flooded inside with worried expressions plastered over them. "We heard someone else coming here! Think that cop called for back-up?"

Zulayka's eyebrows furled together. "We need to get out of here now."

"Not so fast."

Jonah emerged from the door, the vantablack shooter back in its holster and in his right hand a pocket knife gleaming from its fresh meal of rope.

"How'd you get out?" Ish asked, terror pushing his legs back one step.

As a reply, Jonah simply waved around his knife.

The ex-captain stepped forward, sheathing his knife. "Why did you kids come out here?" Confusion pained his voice.

Falaq took the lead. "Zulayka saved us. It's our fault you went after her." After a small pause, Falaq said, "She taught us. If we decided to abandon her, then that would've meant that we had learned nothing."

Jonah turned around to face the door, hiding his expression. A few minutes passed in this silence.

"I see." Jonah pulled out his Shade-eater from his holster once again while touching the gash on his neck with his other hand. "There's no time. The hovercycle's in the back. Some scrap might be enough to serve as a makeshift sled if you tie it right, for the kids."

Ish's mouth fell open.

"Jonah, what are you doing?" Zulayka asked. In those few moments outside alone in the night, something in Jonah had changed.

"You proved me wrong, Zulayka. When I listened to the recordings between you and Abraham, I couldn't bring myself to take him seriously. I've seen betrayal more than sacrifice, despair more than hope. Yet, somehow, here you all are.

"It's her. She's coming, Zulayka. I'm going to ask you for something, though I know I don't deserve it." With shame, Jonah stared at the ground. "Allow me to hold her off. During that time, escape."

Zulayka's gaze softened. On this day, the world would lose

yet another Insurgent. "Goodbye, Jonah." Zulayka said. The others followed in suit. Falaq headed out, unable to keep himself from looking back. Falaq's tears crashed against the floor. There is no tear more sacred than the tear that is shed in the night. They rode away into its sheltering embrace.

Once they were gone, the deserts of Jonah's eyes reached their river. For the first time in so long, he felt his heart be at ease. The Shade-eater rested in his fingers, loaded with his regrets.

The door creaked open. The Supervisor entered, unsurprised by Zulayka's absence.

"You were contaminated, Jonah. What I did was for your own good. This time, stay in your grave." They each drew their guns and fired.

All the Orphans of Kaam heard with their ears were gunshots in the distance.

Entry 5- My mind drifts back to Rabia. I can't help it. It's been years since I've seen her last. I know she's changed so much but I often think back to those days when it was only us five at the start of it all. Isaac believed that the Revolution was a project that revolved around the heart. Isaac knew it was only He who was the changer of hearts. I wonder if Rabia remembers that. How lonely she must be. How isolated from herself. If I called out to her, would she hear me? I know that we are destined to meet again, that I will meet my end when we do. My heart can't help but break. After all, I remember my master Hussein, whose nobility and grace extended to those who strived to make him a martyr. He pleaded with them, begged for them to change their ways, to follow the one and only true path. So many denied him, so many rejected him. But I remember Hur. I remember his love, I remember the beauty of when he reunited with Hussein. With these memories in my heart, I will move forward. There exists nothing more vast than God's mercy.

Signed, Abraham

***

In the unknowable sky, the sun marked the dusk of night, the dawn of day. The seed of Hussein blossomed only under the rains of blood, the air from dying breaths, the rays that shone out most brilliantly against the dark.

Zulayka, Falaq, and Mayar returned to the shallow, skinny river. Its waters fought through the stony dirt, pushing out a path from nothingness. Where the water roamed, life followed. Without water, there was only death. There was only stone.

It is through water that stone is broken. It is through a tear that a heart is healed. It was through a river that a Revolution was born.

***

For a taste of your countenance I'll seek out the night
Since you entered the cloak of light, I crave its sight
The stars envy your endless admirers and sigh
Praying that, like you, one day they'll be up as high
Ode to Hussein, from the collections of Falaq

The Falling Sky

The Falling Sky

From You, 2000 Years Ago

Words are unfit for this tragedy. Ink cannot contain the tears, sounds cannot contain the screams. There are not enough letters to express it, there are not enough pages to transcribe it. A tear shed for the king of hearts becomes an ocean, uncrossable in its magnitude and unknowable in its depths. Praise Him for every tear, for the water needed to birth them. A tear shed in the deserts of Karbala becomes an oasis.

Fissures like deep black cracks split through the rocky earth, their divisions undeniable. However, the schisms of time differ. Slice a pond in half and the whole pond will remain, but what lurked within still felt the tongue of the blade. Ripples cascade across the surface, heading in all directions of the circle of history. It is felt everywhere, all at once. All ripples lead back to the center, all things whisper its name. Such sorrow is not restrained by time or space. Such was the tragedy of Karbala.

The prince's coronation marked by blood and sand was not in vain. He, and the eight that followed him, kept their grandfather's hearth ablaze. They strived in preparation for the Savior, for the Avenger. The one who will rise on Ashura, the one who will avenge his grandfather, the one who will complete the circle of light.

And so we wait, in our own preparation, until his revolution comes.

***

Two decades ago, the Revolution was born. It started with only a tremble, a weak aftershock still humming in the wake of the Insurgency. The Instability Investigation branch, with its ears cupped against the ground, thought nothing of it. To them it seemed like ants crawling out of a hill. Only the Supervisor tried to pursue them, to pin them down, but it was like chasing a falling feather, twirling its way out of her reach, dancing in between her fingers as if to provoke her. Without any proof, her warnings were ignored. Bliss, the Leader of Nardeban, personally ordered her to stop. Bliss kept his arms open and his embrace welcoming to reassure the upper levelers, as a father might hush the worries of his children. Their wounds were too raw, too red, too irritated. Beyond this thorny protection, Bliss' pacifism drew upon an arrogance in the weakness of any movement that would rise against him. His calculated cruelty against the Insurgency was a threat to all who opposed him, one whose face would ward off any resistance. It was a well-timed slap, a thoughtful cutting word to make sure the dissenters knew their place. The sting on their cheek might fade quickly, but Bliss aimed to graze their hearts, their spirits. He thought himself invincible, and his every step marched in tandem with the tyrants of the past, their shadows acting as his mirror. The Supervisor, with the memory of a dying Jonah in her mind, knew better. These were no mere children.

Shielded by Bliss' arrogance, the Revolution planted seeds beneath the concrete. Its roots spread, grasping onto the pockets of light to breathe against walls of suffocating darkness. Cradled by Nardeban's ignorance, the infant rebellion rallied itself across Cities and through the lower levels. With its youth came danger and sensitivity. A slight breeze whipped into a hurricane, a trip tumbled into a fall. The walls closed in around them, and like a hider whose breath rumbles in their ears and whose eyes peer from the small crack of light in the door to see their pursuer approaching, to watch them and hear them as their steps clap against the floor and their figure consumes the hider's whole vision and the air in their lungs scrambles to run away alongside their leaping heart, only for a sigh of relief to crawl out of their throat as the shadow recedes into the distance.

Nardeban was no less insecure. A tower with its weight concentrated at the top is doomed if its base gives way, like a pyramid sitting atop a needle, and the Revolution meticulously sculpted cracks into its foundation. The Instability Investigation branch's scans of different Level 5s were fruitless; they were too drunk on lethargy to detect the Revolution's underground apparatus. Their heads were stuck in the clouds. Since the sky was conquered, the Revolution made use of the land, stealing construction drills and machinery until they built their own. They tunneled their way until they spanned all of Nardeban. Within the earth, all became connected in only a few years as the roots sensed and pushed their way through the soil, seeing without seeing. Those who united the paths of their hearts and the paths of the tunnels were guided to the same destination, the same origin. The new sympathizers of the Insurgency and the old members in hiding throughout Nardeban united behind the Revolution's banner, emblazoned with the insignia of the Day Star, a single light standing as a bastion against all of the night.

That was how the candle fueled by embers and cupped against the wind grew to burn through even the rain. It was a fire of vision that burned away impurity, that burned away everything except their ultimate goal. A story unbound by time and space weaved them closer together than the strings of a flame's heart, a tragedy that served as an undying kindling for their efforts. For the Hussein whose efforts transcended death, whose mission was otherworldly, they fought not only for a cause greater than themselves but for a cause greater than the world itself. The frantic cry of the oppressed stretches far beyond the subjugated citizens of Level 5, for the oppressed are those who are subjected to the injustices of the heart, consumed by a world fleeting and limited by nature. The Revolution broadcasted its message up above, hacking the holo-screens of the upper levels and disseminating a new dream for the sedated walkers. As much as Nardeban tried to cover up the fires, they couldn't eliminate the smoke. The upper levelers were given a taste, a rope thrown down to them, waiting to be caught. Then, Revolutionaries held sessions in secret in Levels 4 and above, connecting to those who felt shackled by their supposed freedom. The pursuits of their lives, what had it given them? Was everything constrained to the here and now, to happiness that was fickle and ephemeral? All that was empty, all the things they lost that they never knew they had, none of it could be forgotten. Their hearts longed for something more without knowing what, and the Revolutionaries offered that knowledge to them. And some accepted. They funneled the Revolutionaries with resources and funds and devotion, igniting a new age of solidarity between the Levels that had not been seen for centuries. It was not a revolution of the lower levelers nor of the upper levelers, nor of the poor nor of the rich, nor of the earth nor of the sky. It was something more.

It took 18 years for the whispers of revolt to snake its way to the top. Chaos followed. Vindicated, the Supervisor began her work anew, and Bliss shed his silk gloves, revealing the iron fist clenched underneath. No revolt in his time, in any time, swayed the upper levelers, those whose every step soared above the clouds. For the first time, Bliss tightened his fist around the upper levelers themselves. Suspicion is a second's worth of fear away from paranoia, and security reforms snowballed into questioning and curfews, intimidation and jailing. The two years leading up the Nardeban Civil War brought Bliss' repression down in full force onto all the levels. Amidst the chaos, Bliss raised the Supervisor to his side, granting her powers over the entire state. Eventually, the reinforced Instability Investigation branch got used to the small tremors, stamping out small pockets of the Revolution wherever they could. So much so that they weren't prepared for the earthquake, an unpredictable acceleration erupting into the Nardeban Civil War. It wouldn't even last a month.

Imagine the Supervisor's surprise when the city of Midan was stormed and taken by Revolutionary forces in only a day. As the Revolutionaries scaled the skies, the war began.

***

The clouds soared underneath her.

Hamsa activated her holo-watch, tapping the green bead on her wrist, and felt a sigh wriggle loose from her lips. Her meeting with the Revolutionaries was set to start soon— her final chance to spy for Nardeban—but they were only making it harder for her to do her job with all these new restrictions. With irritation, Hamsa surveyed the landscape before her.

"Who! Who?" steel owls questioned as they sat perched atop the street lamps, with invisible infrared sensors shooting out of their vision. Human sentries patrolled the streets, enforcing the lockdown of Level 2.

She swiped her holo-watch screen back to the map of their positions, struggling to locate a through-line to sneak her way through. If worse came to worst, she could reveal her ID badge, stamped with General Cyrus' lion insignia, and walk away scot free. Looking back at the time, though, she knew that scenario wasn't realistic. It was too much of a time sink and she'd miss the meeting. And this was one Hamsa couldn't afford to miss.

The military spy donned a black hood fashioned with fibers that distorted steel owl sensors and sprinted forward with sound-absorbing combat boots. For once, the sky was clear, aside from the yellow beams of the owls. No hover vehicles shot through the air, consuming the moon and stars. Never in her whole life had Hamsa seen the upper levels like this. Bliss was tightening his grip to keep the Revolution at bay, but in the process cracks showered in his fingers. All that splintered glass tore at his hands, and his worry bled its way to the upper levelers. None ventured outside, jailed inside their homes with the lights off. For once, everyone, no matter their level, could look up and dare to see the stars.

Her time acting out the role of a Revolutionary worsened her condition. Whenever she thought back to it, her fingers curled into a fist, her ears raged with the roar of a waterfall. The Insurgency took everything from her. Things wouldn't be the same this time.

Lost in her thoughts, Hamsa failed to notice her cloak getting caught by something in the darkness. Before she could process what it was, she felt a cold yellow glare burn into her. The steel owl raised and spread its wings, and shot out a flurry of sharpened iron feathers. Hamsa's body reacted automatically, launched into action by the feathers that chewed their way in her leg with their gutted edges. The owl opened its beak to shriek an alarm, but before it got the chance a charge of light slammed into its metal body, collapsing into a heavy thunk as the owl fell onto the street with an electric groan.

"Down here!" A voice called out from the darkness.

Without pausing to think, Hamsa chased the sound down the alleyway, narrowly avoiding the slicing beam of light.

"Hamsa, it's nice to see you again," the man spoke, his eyes glinting free of the shadows.

Hamsa blinked. "Oh, it's you, David," she replied, recalling his attendance at the previous Revolution meetings.

"Thanks for the save, I'm lucky to have run into another Revolutionary. I would've been toast," she continued gratefully, switching her mask.

David let out a sigh. "We almost lost you there. You need to be more careful."

Hamsa's mouth twitched, but she forced it into a smile. "I will, trust me," she tapped her holo watch and widened her eyes, "It's almost time for the meeting, don't you think we should head out?"

"There's no need to worry about the meeting. It's been cancelled," David said coolly.

He was lying. Hamsa knew it. "Why was it cancelled?" The atmosphere trembled, awaiting for the thunder after the flash.

"Well, you see, there were some threats of moles in the—" in the middle of speaking, David's hand glided over to his pocket. Hamsa's body blasted into formation, fiercely chopping his arm away while unsheathing her own standard issue knife. She lunged toward him, only to lose grip of her leg as all her weight went onto her injured leg, causing her to collapse.

"Hey, calm down," David said with worry, helping her lean up against the wall. "You don't even realize what I was about to take out." Hamsa held her breath while he withdrew an

ID Badge, emblazoned with Cyrus' green lion.

"You were an infiltrator the entire time too? Why was I never informed about this?" she fumed.
"I never knew you were with Cyrus either. But once I learned your name it became obvious," David replied, fully stepping out of the shadows. His trimmed black beard crinkled along the edges of his mouth while his hair was hidden under an army cap.

Hamsa froze.

David continued, "The infamous agent Hamsa, the one who turned in her own Insurgent parents as a child. I suppose it makes sense for a traitor to become a spy."

"And what about it? Would you not have done the same?" Hamsa sneered.

"Of course, I would have done the same. But I didn't have to," he paused and watched the ground thoughtfully, then saying, " It must have been difficult for you, Hamsa." He was taunting her, she thought. Yet all she heard was pity.

Unwillingly, her thoughts drifted back to that day.

***

Her father was a quiet man. Together with her mother they lived a simple life in Level 3, where her father worked as a baker. Each morning in her bed, Hamsa clumsily recalled the shuffling of feet past her door and the yawning groan of the fire in the oven. Bread and sweets greeted her scent when she arose, specially made at home with their centuries old oven instead of at her father's shop. The oven's old brick and clay seemed to pop straight out of her history lessons, the days when mankind still struggled to conquer the earth.

But her father didn't mind it. He told Hamsa it was a good reminder for him, gesturing towards the clay. His fingers strained, wanting to speak more, but the clock stared relentlessly at his neck like the beating of the sun.
The dawn lifted his eyes each day and he lifted his knobby hands up to the kitchen. There they swam into the dough, rippling through its surface. Like wave after wave cresting against the shore, the dough folded in on itself ferociously while the lightning of his hands struck against the mass. Again and again they plunged into the dough until all the white flour, like sea foam, melted back into its undistinguishable layers. When his hands resurfaced, gasping for breath, the kneaded dough shone as if a shimmering lake, still and whole.

After the father shaped the clay and fed it the breath of the air, he thrust it into the fire. The flame's majesty surrounded the vessel, until it birthed a heat of its own within its folds. Something within the dough bubbled up to the surface, singing along the simmering embers. Shaking free from its cocoon, gold burst through from shapeless white, its unrestricted bounds hardening along its border. The fiery alchemist dipped its orange finger into its heart and blazed it awake. The heat transmuted and forged the dough from within, until it rose, lifted only by its faith, and solidified, as sturdy as any mountain.

Satisfied with his work, in a way no other baker was, the father left for his restaurant. At school, Hamsa walked the halls with trepidation, as mentions of the Insurgency hid behind every corner. The word itself was doom, and it spelled annihilation for the upper levels of Nardeban. Their way of life was at stake, both the levels and something more. Some existential dread, some terror their hearts did not know but sensed, something it viciously clung onto to protect. Hamsa and her classmates swallowed down this fear, and it blackened their vision. Amid all that hopelessness, one figure broke through it.

The grim face of then Lieutenant Cyrus glared from every holoscreen. As a spy, Cyrus infiltrated the Insurgency and gained knowledge of all of their bases across Nardeban. In his brilliant act of betrayal after years of pretending to work with the Insurgency, Cyrus would be responsible for the total assault on the Insurgency that would wipe them off the earth. During class, Hamsa watched in awe as Leader Bliss declared Lieutenant Cyrus to be General Cyrus, back while his hair still clung to his head and his scar was fresh on his visage.

Upon returning home to her parents, gloomy eyed after their work, Hamsa excitedly told them about her new dream: to join the Instability Investigation branch and become a spy. They were silent. She didn't understand. They urged her to sleep, promising to talk to her tomorrow.

Hamsa tossed and turned that night, a sick feeling pervading in her stomach. Tomorrow inched forward and yet ran at her. Restless and disturbed, she shook herself up from bed and headed to the bathroom, only to open her door to the breath of the oven burning down into smoke. She entered the kitchen, surprised at the embers still lit. The sounds nagged at her, and she splashed water over the coals, choking the light into a memory. Past the oven's sizzling screams, Hamsa heard whispers outside, the voices of her parents. She peeked out the door leading out of the house to find them there, clutching baskets of bread as if they were bags of gold. With uncertainty hanging onto her as she clung to the night, Hamsa followed them down to Charon's Boat, the elevator that rocketed people through the levels at the speed of shadow. For the first time in her life, Hamsa entered Level 5.

Immediately, she gagged. The putrid air assaulted her nostrils, and each proceeding step became woozier than the last. But she had come too far. Tomorrow would have to wait.

Stumbling in her parent's footsteps, Hamsa dove behind a boulder when she saw others approaching from the distance. A man and a woman. They were both part of the Insurgency, wearing its insignia openly on their clothes. Hatred erupted within her.

Hamsa's parents didn't share her sentiments. They bounded over, embracing the Insurgents. Then, gingerly, her parents handed over the bread. The male Insurgent took one out and carefully broke one apart, revealing a paper hidden inside.

Hamsa stepped back. She ran away, all the way back to Level 3.

A part of Hamsa urged her to return home, to pretend like nothing happened, to wait and listen to what her parents had to say. But the holoscreens of General Cyrus watched her. His bravery taunted her. His glory called out to her. She answered.

Hamsa reported her parents to the Instability Investigation branch. They ransacked her house and they found the intelligence her mom had stolen and they waited for her parents to return. When they did, the agents slammed vantablack cuffs down on their hands, dragging them away. They called out to her, passing on advice to her, worrying over her. She forgot all that they said. She wasn't sure if she ever even listened.

***

Hamsa adjusted her leg. The bleeding was starting to slow down. She turned the iron feather around in her hand absentmindedly, shocking herself back into reality as it shallowly cut her hand.

"Maybe don't play around with the sharp object that just stabbed your leg," David said, quickly removing the blade from her hand.

Hamsa turned her face away from him.

"I wasn't kidding about the meeting being cancelled, though."

She whipped her head back, "Does that mean we're not going to learn the Revolution's next target? How can you say that so calmly?"

David sighed. "Relax. I already got the info we needed." David steeled his voice, "They're going to liberate the City of Kaam."

Hamsa gasped. They were going to strike at her home.

***

"What are we going to do?" Bliss asked. He stood at the spearhead of his palace, miles from the ground, in the capital of Pyra. Like the pharaohs of old, he commanded from atop an obsidian pyramid, the largest structure both in Nardeban and the world. "We need to put a stop to this now," he said, veins strikingly clear on his head.

Midan was still under rebel control, surviving the government's siege by using their own weapons against them. The Revolutionaries created improvised weapons, weapons that Nardeban's army held no defenses for. The anxiety of upper levelers everywhere reached a fever pitch as the hopes of Revolutionaries flared higher.

"Midan was only the beginning, you know that. It's only a matter of time—" the Supervisor was cut off by the thunderous approach of General Cyrus, his footsteps echoing off of the pitch black marble floor.

Out of all of Midan's generals, Cyrus was the oldest and the strangest. Rumors spoke of his ascent from the lower levels, like the Supervisor herself. His short stature seemed to corroborate this, along with his knowledge of the lower levels. Great efforts were taken to keep his past under wraps.

"Leader Bliss, I have urgent news. Our spies have given word that the Revolutionaries are planning to invade the city of Kaam next, three days from now," the general smiled and the scar crossing over his lips widened, "But we have the advantage. We know where their encampment is, official dockets from Kaam's Instability Investigation branch confirmed it. I can end this tonight."

"Provide the spy's report right away to the Instability Investigation branch's headquarters," Bliss instructed with glee. "You've outdone yourself once again, Cyrus. Looks like the Supervisor's recommendation paid off twice."

"Of course, Leader Bliss. Cyrus understands what's at stake. After all, that's why he betrayed the Insurgency." The Supervisor fondly turned towards the general, "Hurry with delivering those reports to my office, please. They might be hiding more than the ordinary eye can see."

Cyrus nodded. "Understood, ma'am," but Cyrus redirected his attention to Leader Bliss, adding,"There's one more thing, though. I request permission to take the Pyra's Capital Guard along with me to obliterate the rebels."

Some mechanical rumble rippled through the pyramid. Bliss stayed completely still, contemplating. The Capital Guard was his own elite fighting force. Each year, select citizens in Levels 3 and 2 offered their children to the capital in exchange for earning the privilege of ascending the levels. Their children, too, rose to Level 1, subjected to years of training. Alongside the grueling physical exercise, Bliss took care to drill into them Nardeban's philosophy. He instructed them on the five levels, the delicate nature of Nardeban's peace, and their role in preserving it. Their reshaped identities, hammered out like steel, afforded the Capital Guard an unrivaled loyalty among the military. Though they were used more for show than battle, their strength was unparalleled thanks to certain modifications. The Capital Guard was barely human, their bodies a blend of flesh and steel. Gazing over the portraits of previous Nardeban Leaders, Bliss replied, "Go ahead and take your own forces, General Cyrus, and deal with them like we did the Insurgency. However," Bliss narrowed his eyes, "I will absolutely not leave the capital undefended. Pyra's guards will remain—"

"That won't cut it, Bliss. The tech they have isn't like anything we've seen. Our vantablack weapons get completely nullified by their shield systems. If I go without the capital guard, we'll lose Kaam and it'll be a massacre. Is that something we can afford?" Was it a question, or a challenge? Bliss' eyes widened at Cyrus' indignation.

"What can be given can just as easily be taken away, General. Speak too quickly and you'll find yourself tripping over your own words," Bliss said, with an edge to his tone.

"The situation is dire, Leader Bliss, that is all I wish to express. The upper levelers are terrified as it is, between the Revolutionaries taking Midan and your own security measures sinking them deeper into panic. I need the chance to remind this Revolution of the Insurgency's devastation from 20 years ago, to gift them a fear that'll keep these rabbits in their burrows."

Burrows, the Supervisor thought. Her mind flashed scenes of another life, running through those tunnels with Abraham and Naamah, the dead body clutched in her hands. No one knew about those days except for her and Bliss; Cyrus was too young.

"Damn it," Bliss whispered. He turned away from the stares of his predecessors. Their dark legacy burned through him. Losing Midan *and* Kaam would be a humiliation. Nardeban wasn't under any real threat of losing this pathetic excuse of a civil war, but it needed a total victory, undeniable domination. Trust was forged from fire, and only carnage would win back the upper levelers through fear and awe. More than survival, psychology was at stake. Bliss knew the rebels wouldn't dare to strike Pyra. It was the impregnable citadel, the unyielding fortress. Even if they did siege, the Capital Guards weren't his only form of defense anymore. His latest magnificent creation was unknown to either General Cyrus or the Supervisor, one that would take care of the Revolution if all else failed. All the cards remained safely in Bliss' hands.

The Supervisor intervened. "Bliss, there's no reason to take this risk. Keep the Capital Guard here, the Revolution won't withstand the might of Cyrus' forces—"

"Take them," Bliss curtly told Cyrus. His word was final. The Supervisor glared.

"You won't regret this, Bliss." Cyrus exited the chamber, nostalgia simmering in his heart as the memories of the old Insurgency flowed through him. By nightfall, General Cyrus and his army would arrive at Kaam to wipe out the Revolution.

***

Falaq sat at his withering desk, pen glistening while the paper lying before him remained blank and unfilled. A drought plagued his fingers and no words flooded into his mind. His canvas was parched for a taste of wisdom. He sighed. The faucet of his fingers was shut tight. There was something within him waiting to be written, like the sounds of water running beneath the earth, but he couldn't dig his way through the ground. All he could do was listen, until the doors opened when they were ready. Once the moment arrived, his skill could draw out light from the darkest of ink.

Falaq abruptly rose from his seat, tossing a crumpled sheet into the waste bin. Walking outside his hastily set up tent, he waved to Ishmael and the other Revolutionaries. His face brightened as he saw the children play outside, free from the gas masks of his youth. Mayar and his team managed to cook up the machinery needed to purify the air enough for their safety. Falaq recalled the steaming wreckages of prototypes with blackened pipes twisted senselessly by strain and rainbows of wires shot open by beams of white light. The final contraption itself was ingenious, tapping into the pollution itself and recasting it into cleanliness. Mayar once spent painstaking hours going over the designs with Falaq before he completed it. The machine's form was based on the long extinct cypress tree. Its strong trunk protruded from the earth and showered into bundles of synthetic and permeable branches covered in leaves. Iteration after iteration, however, only produced failures. Individually, each machine used up too much power and blew apart under the strain of cleaning the air. So Falaq passed on a simple suggestion.

"Why don't you just add roots? It already looks like a tree anyways," Falaq told Mayar absentmindedly.

After days of drought, Mayar's soul reawakened from that single drop and he wordlessly sped off into the distance. Stumped, Falaq thought nothing of it until one day when he stepped out of his tent, forgetting his gas mask inside.

He sniffed. Hesitantly, at first, like a nervous hand reaching underneath the darkness of a couch afraid of what it may find. Then, eagerly. He breathed shallowly, then quickly, then deeply, with tears streaming down. The air was clean.

He was surrounded by trees.

To keep the power from short circuiting each individual tree, Mayar added a root system that connected all the units together, boosting efficiency while lowering the total power needed and reducing strain by dividing it across the grid. The leaves took in the polluted air, sang it through the trunk where it was stripped of impurity, and exhaled the rest back from the roots.

The iron tree was the beginning of much more. It inspired Mayar to modify Nardeban's vantablack tech, which converted darkness into solids, into light bearing ones. His model expanded off of the design of vantablack cuffs and Shade-eaters, the plasma-like shadow that gave the cuffs and bullets their incredible resilience needed only a few simple yet ingenious adjustments to create solid light. These light-tech guns tapped into the radiance surrounding them and fashioned it into pearl bullets. The tools of bondage and war transformed into a chance for liberation. Wherever there existed corruption, they held the ability to take it within themselves and craft purity. It was Mayar's way of bringing Zulayka's lessons into his work, to craft pearls from dirt and shade.

The flag of the Day Star puffed up with breaths of wind passing through its chest. The nostalgia from returning to Kaam after almost twenty whole years of running and organizing from City to City slammed into him. Falaq's eyes were guided to the sky. It was a rare night where the moon glowed all the way down to Level 5, and he felt its mystery reach out and touch his heart. A crescent that stood for infinite growth, still young in the clouds as the sun subsided into sleep only moments earlier. Like the ocean tide, the moon compelled the words inside him to rise.

His writing would have to wait. Jolting Falaq's awareness, an alarm blared throughout the camp, as enemy hoverships came from the horizon. They were practically flying stadiums, three in total with one marked by the capital insignia of an obsidian pyramid, one other with the five barred flag of Kaam, and the last branded with the personal symbol of Cyrus, the mythical lion, extinct for a thousand years.

"Ishmael, are you ready?" Falaq asked, stepping towards him. Ish nodded. The two looked out into the crowd.

"I wonder if this is what it looked like the first time Nardeban clamped down on Kaam." Ishmael wondered out loud. He was thinking about his parents. He was peering out at all the worried faces of the children, all certain of their incoming doom. His heart wanted to reach out and reassure them, but he held himself back. Falaq watched him carefully.

Falaq replied softly, "Make sure the others who know what's

coming don't cause any info leaks, especially when we're this close to the operation. Prepare for a surrender." Falaq smiled. "A surrender that will take down all those airships in one blow."

***

"Revolutionaries!" General Cyrus announced from the capital ship's sound amplifier, "Surrender yourselves, or face the full brunt of the Nardeban army." His voice boomed across all of Level 5.

Hamsa hid her grin. There was no way out for the Revolution. Trigger happy, she reached for the button to begin fire, but the general's hand clamped down on her wrist, causing her to yelp. Before she could question him, he already walked away with his stern shadow trailing behind him. Hamsa bit her tongue. One way or another, no one from that camp was going to survive.

Aboard the incoming fleet, General Cyrus commanded all troops to withhold fire, restraining the overwhelming bloodlust pouring forth from their hungry gazes.

"Hold! Take the time to break their morale, to let the terror sink in deeper than the bullets do. Remember to keep the cameras rolling. This'll be a night to remember." Cyrus kept glancing at his watch.

Down on the ground, Falaq and the others put their hands up, gathering Revolutionary soldiers and children alike. It was an unconditional surrender. The Revolutionary invasion was foiled.

"What's *that*?" One commander suddenly yelled, her finger pointing to their scanner. A dozen scarlet red circles spawned on the screen, completely surrounding the imperial legion.

"That," Cyrus said as he aimed his gun towards the commander, "is the Revolutionary fleet surrounding us." The captain led the mutiny. It was his finest betrayal to date. Hundreds followed suit across all three ships, with hidden Revolutionaries circling state soldiers and uncovering their pins marked by the Day Star. David rose and pointed his own weapon to Hamsa.

"You… and Cyrus… you're both traitors? You're both Revolutionaries?" Hamsa asked, spitting out each word with revulsion and confusion.

David only cocked his gun in response.

Hamsa looked towards General Cyrus. She frantically searched for some sign, a smirk, a knowing glance, anything to change the catastrophic failure facing her. But Cyrus' eyes, for the first time since she met him, flamed with sincerity.

Hamsa stared down the barrel of the gun and filled herself with conviction. "For Nardeban! For Leader Bliss!" she screamed, slamming down on the button to fire before David could react. A boom rocketed through the hovership, smoke covering the windowed view of the earth below, and she laughed as the traitors shoved her against the window.

"Take another look, Hamsa," David said.

A shimmering shield rebounded the blast as a spiralling ring of Revolutionaries vessels closed in on them. In one foul swoop, the offensive was broken from the inside. Hamsa fell into despair, Kaam fell into the hands of the Revolutionaries.

The battalion landed and the Revolutionaries escorted the newly made prisoners of war outside. Spies from the Revolutionaries' own ranks were purged. Thanks to Cyrus, the Revolutionaries knew which spies were allied with Nardeban and which spies were with them. Falaq headed towards the prisoners, pausing as one heated Revolutionary butted heads with a prisoner.

As her hands were restrained with vantablack cuffs by a Revolutionary, Hamsa snidely called out to him, "Don't touch me with your filthy hands, *abysswalker*." Bitterness brimmed in the final word.

"What did you just say to me?" he responded angrily. As they each prepared to engage, Falaq put himself between them, but it was too late. Their altercation set off the tension already sparking. A vocal portion of Kaam's Revolutionaries verbally blasted out against the now defenseless crowd.

"We're not going to give them any of our supplies! Not that they'd want any of our filthy food regardless!"

"These poisoners don't deserve to walk on our land, not after what they dumped into it."

"Everyone," Falaq's voice cut through the venom. His fury emanated strongly enough for the Revolutionary who struck the prisoner to step back. "Everyone," he repeated, "have you learned nothing?"

"Our goal today is not to lash out at defenseless people. Neither it is about escaping our anger; it is about knowing what to be angry at. It is about knowing injustice and justice, it is about transcending from a rebellion against the outside world to a revolution against the world within. When you hear these upper levelers launch their insults at you, know that they are a reflection of who you all once were, and who you still could be if you fail to alter the injustice hidden in your hearts. They are led by someone far crueler who truly deserves your hatred. Choose cruelty now, and it won't matter if we take every City. It won't matter if we feed and clothe and house every person. Stain yourself now, and that stain will burden any future you hope to create. The future is born from the conduct of our actions today, there is no such thing as a bright shadow. Remember yourselves, remember Hussein, remember the Savior." His tone grew gentle, as he asked, "Or have you forgotten? Have you forgotten that Zulayka herself, one of our highest members, is an upper leveler? Have you forgotten that this operation was only made possible thanks to help from spies from Nardeban's army, like General Cyrus and his soldiers? Have you forgotten that the message entrusted to you is meant for all of humanity, is meant to uplift all those who live and breathe, not just us lower levelers?" Falaq's vision pierced into their souls, viewing the same indignation that once roared through him, the same animosity he pitted to Zulayka when they first met.

The soldier who incited the near riot immediately apologized, shame rolling down his bowed back. At the core of Falaq's fury was his love. Before the Revolution, no one valued the people they were, no one protected and fostered their characters in a way that put themselves first. The Revolutionaries' respect for Falaq ran deeper than the Kaam river, and their trust stretched across wider. Together, they cried out, "For the Revolution!"

Falaq whispered a prayer of gratitude. The prisoners behind him weren't sure how to react. They didn't expect this. All the holographic footage they viewed, the battle scenarios they drilled up on, the strategies they painstakingly planned, none of it prepared them for this. Hamsa could only think of Cyrus. She cried, remembering the last words her parents called out to her.

"Wait for us."

Falaq left the two factions there, making his way back to the tent before he himself left Kaam for the final battle. There, General Cyrus sat waiting for him, tears sparkling in his eyes like stars. The two embraced.

"We really did it," Cyrus finally spoke.

"It was thanks to you, Cyrus. It was thanks to your patience."

"Do you know my story, then? Do you know who I am?"

"Parts," Falaq replied, "but not all of it."

Cyrus backed into his chair, gazing through the crack of the tent that revealed the glowing hand of the moon. "It was many decades ago. I joined the Insurgency when Abraham became its leader. Isaac's death left a pall over those who remained. But Abraham was everything he was, and it wasn't long before the Insurgency grew to even greater heights."

The mention of Abraham's name brought distress to his worn heart. Abraham's execution was etched into his mind. "Abraham himself asked me to join Nardeban's army. I was outraged. It was the only time I ever questioned him. What he said to me back then wasn't too different to what you said to all those Revolutionaries outside right now. There was something I couldn't see that he could. And if I ever wanted to look through his eyes, I needed to accept that."

The ex-general's words quieted. The scars on the moon ached.

"Your loyalty was strong enough to follow your leader when you knew you had to. You joined Nardeban's army, what happened next?" Falaq said, placing a shoulder over the old man's taut shoulder.

"Yes, I joined. I accepted my mission, my role. The darkness surrounded me day and night. But the worst was yet to come. One day, Abraham contacted me for the first time since I had gone undercover, since I went under Rabia's wing. He told me…"

Falaq's vision fell to the ground.

Cyrus gathered himself, and continued. "He told me to reveal the location of Kaam. He said the bases were already compromised. There was a traitor in his inner circle, and they found out too late. No matter what, the Insurgency was doomed. He told me to give up Kaam first, to raise my status in Nardeban. I asked him why. I pleaded with him. I begged him. He held my hand and asked me to wait. To wait as long as necessary. To wait until others would rise up, and finish the mission he held dearest to his heart. I did not deny him this. I could not deny him this. Out of love for him, I destroyed the Insurgency at Kaam. They all knew it was coming. Your parents, the parents of all the Orphans of Kaam, used their time not to protect themselves but to ensure that all your lives would be spared. Their sacrifice, all for my false ascension."

"You sacrificed everything for the Insurgency, for Abraham, Cyrus. Tell me, now, how long you waited."

"For more than two decades after Kaam, more than two

decades after the Insurgency, more than two decades after I witnessed my teacher's death, I waited. For all those years, I hid my light in the darkness, I hid my candle in the shadow. I prayed each and every night for just a single day."

Uncontrollably, water surged from Cyrus' eyes.

Falaq rose to the curtain folds of the tent. "That day has come. That night will end." He looked back at the ex-general. "You did well, Cyrus. Your patience will be rewarded, your heart knows it. Now, evil shall curse your name and righteousness will honor it. All things fall into their place."

"That is justice," Cyrus finished. Falaq exited the tent, leaving Cyrus with his thoughts and the cleared air.

Walking by the River of Kaam, Falaq spoke into his communicator.

"Kaam is ours, everything went according to plan."

"You've taken back your home, and I've taken back mine. Bliss doesn't have as much time as he thinks he does. Come join us soon, once we retake the Capital of Pyra and overthrow Nardeban," a jubilant voice crackled back. The battle rapidly neared its end.

"I will, Zulayka." Falaq balled his fist in feverish excitement, sharing a knowing smile with the moon. A quiet rain splattered across his cheeks. It was time for him to set off for the capital to join Mayar and Zulayka. The Revolution was ascending upon them.

***

The city of Pyra loomed before the Revolutionary army,

each level occupying distinct levels and coming together into an obsidian black triangle. It sent chills down their spine, a crimson eeriness bleeding through the air. Every capital has its own unique feature, something that raises its status, a testimony to its larger role. Pyra's distinctive characteristic was that there was no longer any Level 5. Not after Bliss took it upon himself to raze it to the ground and make it uninhabitable for any aspiring rebel group after the Insurgency.

Zulayka saw the anxiety trickling through her Revolutionaries as the battle wound closer. She addressed them, carrying the banner of the Day Star in her hand and lifting it above her with the same arm tied with a black scrap of hijab, causing a hush to sweep through the gathering.

"Today we aim to conquer the capital. 20 years ago it seemed impossible. 5 years ago it seemed impossible. 1 year ago it seemed impossible. But here we are nonetheless, for it is only He who determines what is possible and impossible. Once again, let us ask ourselves: why have we come here? Why have we fought battle after battle, risked our lives, some who have risked their luxurious livelihoods in the upper levels, and others who have risked to strike back even after being shown the brutality of Nardeban in destroying their efforts? Why? What brings us together, from throughout Nardeban and across the levels? It is because of the sacrifice of the one who gave his life, the lives of his family, and the lives of his companions for the sake of the truth. The one truth, the one mission, the one light.

"As we wait for the Avenger, the one who slices the neck of injustice and pierces the heart of evil, we will prepare. We will prepare by forging a new state from the still-warm ashes of the old. In order to achieve this, we must realize our unity, and the unity of the world. We must realize that our enemies are but the wave, and we are the ocean that will swallow them up. For this cause, to purify yourself, prepare to give away everything and prepare to be left with nothing. That in itself is a blessing. The one who has nothing has everything, for they realize that there is nothing but Him, and He is everything. Those of you who still doubt, those of you who still fear, doubt not and fear not. Purge these things from your vision, purge them from every corner and crevice, purge them from every cell in your body. Because of the darkness of the night, do you doubt the rising of the sun? If the sun will not rise, then we shall make a falling sky. Because of the storm clouds of yesterday, do you fear the roaring rains of tomorrow? If the flooding showers arrive, then we will be the fire that burns away the rain. If you hear the horn of death calling to you, then answer. There is no greater blessing than martyrdom in His Name. There is no one closer to the light than one who dies for it, who becomes immortal from it, who loses their whole self in the enchanted hunt for it. May the martyrs who are born today, live on in the hearts of those who survive. Let the Battle for Pyra begin. For the Revolution!"

"For the Revolution!" Thousands of voices yelled back, rippling through the massive crowd, acting as one. The Revolution's uppercut strategy went into play, to tear their way through all the levels until they pierced through its head. The Revolutionary army broke through the belly of the beast and took formation around the center of the level. At the core of each center stood one elevator.

Despite their intelligence saying that the Capital Guards were captured at Kaam, a formidable segment of them remained at Pyra, and reacted as if they knew the attack was coming. Mayar noticed and bit his lip. Either traitors from the Revolutionary base at Kaam or some state spy that managed to pass the vetting in their own ranks sold them out just minutes ago.

Twilight settled on the battlefield as the Capital Guard rocketed off giant orbs of shadow. They let loose their Shade-eater cannons and rifles, showering the sky with a wall of darkness. The abyss shot straight down.

"Activate the shields!" Mayar yelled. In an instant, a blinding sheet of light vaporized the incoming fleet of gloom. Back in his throne room, Bliss' mouth fell agape.

"Return fire!"

The Revolutionaries charged their light weapons, taking in the heart of the moon, and fired. The waves of solid light refracted into a rainbow onslaught, shooting its arrow into the panicking enemy.

Without warning, the Capital Guard retreated above through Charon's Boat, leaving Level 4 completely deserted. "Let's keep going!" Mayar shouted, and the Revolutionaries advanced up to Level 3 in the Capital Guards' footsteps. With each level they climbed, the space grew thinner and taller as the Revolution closed in on the top of the pyramid. The buildings soared higher, the opulence flashed with its dull brilliance.

The level was unnervingly empty but the air was filled with the sound of a threatening hum. Everyone evacuated in a rush before the Revolution's surprise strike, evident by the unlocked doors and glittering mess in the streets. The humming intensified.

"What's going on?" Zulayka questioned Mayar. A horde of robots answered.

Dozens shot out from the unoccupied buildings and alleyways, others descending from the level above. They were vantablack, feeding upon the darkness of the night. Their husks were forged from shade and steel, otherworldly phantoms without will.

Bliss watched on his holoscreen, not realizing the Supervisor had left his side. His final trump card was in play. The secret he never told that traitor, Cyrus.

"T-that's impossible, our spies told us those should still be under development… There's no way," Mayar stammered, and Zulayka flashed him a look, probing for more information. "Pyra's engineers must have perfected it in secret. It's the Automated Army system. They're programmed to kill and function as a completely synchronized force, literally armored by solid darkness. That's not all. Look at the Capital Guards."

The mechanized bodies of the Capital Guards were freezing in place, dying into darkness, and reviving in perfect coordination with the robots. The last bits of their flesh corrupted into an ugly, deep purple, and the night grew darker. "They must have adjusted the cybernetic components implemented into the bodies of the Capital Guard to work in tandem with the Automated Army. We're not fighting anything remotely close to human. Their reaction time must be near instantaneous." The darkness in their hearts became manifest.

The Automated Army growled as they zipped through the urban battlefield. Flying gunships with impeccable accuracy to mow down enemies, steel-furred berserkers designed to roll and ram into crowds and weaponry to destroy them with its sheer speed, instinct driven and animalistic tanks equipped with sonic-barrels sending shockwaves of sound to disorient any enemy unit. It was an unstoppable force. Just as they closed in on the Revolutionaries, still standing firm against the upcoming onslaught, they all stopped at once. A massive holoscreen covered the sky above, with Leader Bliss's glare shooting down.

"Surrender. You have no chance against the Automated Army. If you choose to fight, then I'll use them to wipe out Revolutionary forces everywhere in Nardeban. Not a single one of you will be allowed to survive. Every Level 5 everywhere will be razed to the ground and remade into the utopia Nardeban was always meant to be." A gleeful smirk plastered its way over his face. Their attack on the capital was a surprise, but all it accomplished was giving him free test subjects and media glory. Everyone would witness the fall of the Revolution.

There was not a moment of hesitation from the Revolutionaries. The response came in an overwhelming cry of gunfire with Mayar's light-tech pushed to its absolute limit. The holoscreen shut off with a disgruntled Bliss, and the Automated Army retaliated.

"Mayar, you need to find a way to stop those things. If not, then the Revolution ends here," Zulayka instructed him calmly. His face instantly paled. "No pressure or anything," she said jokingly to loosen his nerves. With a certainty beyond faith, she told him "Trust in Him and everything will go on as it needs to." She fondly recalled her last few talks with Abraham. He was with her at this moment too. Mayar breathed deeply and concentrated on the robots, visualizing the scenario before him. "Even though they're autonomous, they need to be tied back to something. After all, everything is linked to its source. I'll take my tech team and hound out the spot, it must be somewhere on this level. Are you and your squad going to start heading up?"

Despite the situation, Zulayka found herself smiling at the young man she met so long ago now. His light now guided the Revolution forward. "I'm proud of you, Mayar." Taken off guard, Mayar found himself smiling back. "Do what you need to do, I'm off." Directing a few members to accompany her, Zulayka slipped away into the chaos, her objective to find and subdue Bliss and end this battle as soon as she could. She trusted in Mayar as she trusted in herself. Weaving her way through the battle, Zulayka lended assistance however she could as she sped through on her hovercycle. Mayar tinkered on it, installing plenty of new upgrades capable of blasting through the mechanical carnage before her, and her accompaniment traveled close behind on their own vehicles. The biggest obstacle was the wave of steel-furred berserkers, tank-sized land vehicles that were charging forward like a roll of spiked armadillos. These metal beasts were relentless, never slowing down.

Down. Zulayka realized something and stared at the unstable floor of Level 3 below. An idea burst through.

"Drill!" Zulayka commanded. The soldiers looked back at her blankly. "You should all still have a light-drill from when we constructed our underground network. Start drilling into the floor. You don't need to go too deep, it just needs to be wide enough to stop those berserkers in it, then they'll do the rest of the work." A series of hopeful nods replied and they set to work digging.

"Brace yourselves," she said, and they stood their ground. This time when the berserkers returned they burrowed into the giant potholes. Trapped in the hole, the berserkers were forced to continue rolling through the earth with their undeniable strength, digging themselves straight through the ceiling of Level 4 and crashing down against the earth. Helping with other minor crises along the way, Zulayka decided to leave her team behind to fend off the Autonomous Army. Zigzagging through the obstacles, Zulayka arrived at Charon's Boat, leading to Level 2. Zulayka entered the elevator.

The Supervisor was waiting for her at the top.

***

"Mayar, I think I found the control room." Mayar and the rest scrambled towards the voice, and were greeted by an array of holoscreens.

"So it *was* up in the attic of Level 3's Administration Chamber," another remarked. Each City in Nardeban contained an Administration Chamber in its Level 3, a center managing processes throughout the entire City. It was the heart of the City, the core of the Capital.

The room's last occupant exited in a rush, with papers stumbling over each other on the desk and a chair helplessly knocked over. The Autonomous Army program was running in front of them, the chips inside the desk that served as a massive harddrive were steaming and grumbling to run all the machines at once. All the veins of the City traced back here.

Picking up the fallen seat, Mayar wheeled himself up to the command console. He started by trying to take control of the robots remotely. The wall of shifting numbers that glew up in front of him made any attempt of that futile. Neither he nor anyone on his squad had the skills to break through this type of security.

If he couldn't take control of them, there might be a way to directly shut them off. He searched and searched but nothing panned out. Frustration dripped into him bit by bit, crossing off option after option. His breaths became short, his body grew rigid, his voice whipped his teammates in a vain effort to discover anything. In the corner of their eyes, the camera feed displayed the bloody scene. The combined forces of the Capital Guards and Autonomous Army were pushing down on the Revolutionary army.

It didn't work. Nothing worked. Mayar closed his eyes and scrunched up his face tightly, biting down on his lip until it bled from concentration. He needed to calm down. His memories sailed him away from the control room, away from Pyra, and back to Kaam, so many years ago.

***

"I can't do it," said an anguished Mayar. "I don't know how." He spent weeks tampering with his prototype drill. Trial after trial, he couldn't break through the primary obstacle, converting the solid light he managed to create into usable energy. Zulayka and the Revolutionary council gave him the task months ago. Precious time dripped by. Without the finished version of the drill, the Revolution's plan to create an underground base was lost. Soon, Nardeban would encounter their growing force, and they'd suffer the same fate as the Insurgency paved their path for them.

"Maybe you do," Zulayka replied. The two sat at the same stream where Falaq and Mayar spent their first lesson with Zulayka. The sound of the running water soothed him. The stream has grown since they last arrived there. It would become a river.

"What do you mean, Miss Zulayka?"

"Think over all you've learned. What I've taught you isn't

only for times of introspection and reflection. The knowledge within you is meant for every circumstance and situation. You've arrived at the next step of your journey, Mayar. Knowledge is only truly known when it is acted upon."

***

"So act upon it," present Mayar repeated. His mind drifted to the city itself. Within the capital, within any city, there existed interconnected systems. Sewers attached to homes leading to waste and treatment plants, pipes to bring in fresh water, wires to tie every process to power. Even the invisible lines between a simple remote and a holovision, all things were connected together. Beyond that, all things reflected the One. Connection. Everything required connection. That's when a solution struck Mayar like lightning. He was literally at the connection. The console itself was the center of the city. If he wasn't skilled enough to turn off the robots behind the advanced firmware, then he'd take a crack at attacking the basic defenses on the city controls. What better way to get rid of pirates than to sink their ship?

"Lights out," Mayar said, turning off the power of the entire city and listening to the groans of dying machines, leaving the smiling moon to light up the path from above.

***

"After two decades, we finally see each other again," the Supervisor declared, brandishing a vantablack gun. The years left her hair gray and body frail, though Zulayka knew the Supervisor's skill in combat remained unmatched.

Zulayka stayed silent, aiming her own weapon. The Supervisor's eyes narrowed on Zulayka's arm tied around with that cloth. At first glance, it was just an inconspicuous black bandana, but she knew better. The faded green scarf lived on in her memory.

"How did you manage to find Zahra's hijab?" she asked Zulayka, an edge to her voice.

Zulayka glanced at the torn scarf, slowly acknowledging its origin. "I found it the same day I left Midan."

"Whatever, it's not like it matt—" the Supervisor cut herself off and shot a zooming shadow that blasted the gun out of Zulayka's hands.

Zulayka gritted her teeth with shock as she clutched her bleeding left hand, a wince of pain forming on her face.

"All alone, aren't you? That was naive, Zulayka. I have no reason to play fair," the Supervisor scolded, stepping forward. "Do you recognize this weapon?" She twirled the Shade-eater around in her hands, and chuckled at Zulayka's grimace. "It was Jonah's. I'll admit, that day you managed to shock me. His defecting was something I didn't expect. Neither did I expect Cyrus to be Abraham's pawn this entire time. Abraham never used to be the type to think so far ahead into the future. These past few years of back and forth have been quite insightful. For that, I thank you." Zulayka clutched her hands together, trying to stem the blood loss.

"That must hurt, doesn't it? The pain you're feeling now was *so* avoidable." A step forward.

"Instead, you wandered all the way here, propelled by some tale pedalled by that ancient grandmother." And another.

"Don't be fooled by your progress. If you can even call it that. I've seen 'Revolutionaries' before. They're all the same." Closer and closer.

"You claim they're giving themselves over to something

greater than themselves. Not that the Revolutionaries actually believe that. They are doomed, and neither of us can change that." Only a few more.

"At the end of the day, they want what's best for them. The levels won't go away. These lights, these *idols* as you'd call them, they'll stay as strong as ever. The heart of man is nothing if not corruptible. People are only free when they fight for themselves and protect those they care about. When they protect those who are like you and I, those who can see, those who can know. No one else." They met each other's eyes, a few feet apart.

"Goodbye, dreamer. Good night," The Supervisor said. There was something in her voice.

Empowered by an otherworldly speed, Zulayka rocketed her right fist towards the Supervisor, who caught it with her left easily, amused at the attempt. That instant of distraction birthed opportunity, as a bloodied left fist blitzed across the Supervisor's cheek, causing her to shoot wildly towards the ground as Zulayka ran away and gained distance.

The nerve to punch with Zulayka's own shot up hand when it should be impossible to close it into a fist irritated the Supervisor. She futilely wiped away at the warm blood on her cheek. She underestimated Zulayka again. Suddenly, the street lights around them flickered off. Zulayka knew it must've been Mayar's doing. In the unblemished night, all the stars break free. All the lights in the night sky were stars.

"I think I understand you now, Rabia," Zulayka began, cutting in and out of the shadows while the Supervisor rapidly rotated, trying to lock in on her position in the darkness. "For all these years, your story always eluded me.. How did someone who founded and worked for the Insurgency for years end up so deep in her animosity against it? Going as far as to slaughter her old friends?" Zulayka's voice transformed into a taunting phantom, regrets dancing along the shadows of the open street. Try as she might, the Supervisor couldn't see an opening.

"Don't call me that name again," the Supervisor hissed, partly from anger and partly as an attempt to provoke a response to pinpoint Zulayka's location.

"Many things cause people to be lost in this world," Zulayka went on. The Supervisor's ears twitched. "And all signs of misguidance come back to signs of guidance that were twisted. All false loves drive back to the true love they deviated from. A love for wealth, a love for glory. But these weren't what deceived you, were they?" questioned Zulayka. The Supervisor tried to ignore her, realizing that Zulayka was no longer circling around her. The Supervisor readied her vantablack arm again.

"No, what misdirected you was another false love that veiled you from Him. You allowed them to become your center and focus, when the only center and the only focus is meant to be Him. Zahra, your father. Your love wasn't aligned to Him, and it unwittingly became a tool against you. You never understood Hussein's tragedy. What he was meant to sacrifice. First, he sacrificed his companions. Then, he sacrificed his family. Finally, once every other layer was stripped away, he sacrificed himself." The Supervisor pressed one hand against her ear, a furious scowl wrinkling across her time-wearied face.

"The heart of man, they say, can only love one. The martyr king did not sacrifice his life to protect his family. He did not sacrifice his life for his friends. It was for Him and no one else. Do not confuse 'love for' and 'love through,' dear Rabia. Indeed he held love for his family and companions, but it was a love channeled through Him. If you are willing to listen now, then there's still a chance." The Supervisor steadied her aim. The hands of evil plugged her ears and further blackened her heart.

"It is through Him we love. We love anything which reminds us of Him in our hearts. Nothing can come first. One does not love a scent because of its flower, they love the flower because of its scent. You claim that life is meant to protect those you care about. Then guard them by guarding the very traits that made you care for them, preserve the light that brought you together. The memory of Zahra and your father, of their eternal lives after this world, those are the same memories you've spent your life soiling. Can't you see it?"

"Enough!" The Supervisor screamed, pulling the trigger and shooting a pellet of shade that tore its way through the layers of darkness.

She heard a thud against the ground and Zulayka's silence. Quaking with emotion, the Supervisor walked over to the body, announcing, "It's over."

Her frenzied thoughts froze her reaction time, the Supervisor's eyes watching the would-be corpse smack her weapon out of her hand and slam on a pair of light cuffs. Squinting, the Supervisor saw that her shot did make contact, on Zulayka's left arm directly atop the remains of Zahra's scarf. The Supervisor's legs crumbled beneath her. The unleashed stars poured down their judgement. While she was left in the dark side of its face, the full moon bled gold over Zulayka.

The Supervisor was too stunned to say anything, forced to watch Zulayka march onwards towards Level 1. For the first time in more than three decades, Rabia cried. It was a rippling wail, soaking in insanity and dripping in regret. She wondered how things became like this. It was Abraham who came to her, who found her. He knew he would be captured, he knew he would be in that cell. That day Rabia and Abraham made a simple bet. He asked the Supervisor to send Zulayka over to him as an interrogator. To hold a test on whose truth was the Truth. It was that fatal bargain that initiated the sequence which led up to her ultimate failure, lying broken at the steps of Level 1. Abraham won. Isaac won. Everything came undone.

***

For the first time in her life, Zulayka arrived in the Capital's Level 1. By now she was so high up that she couldn't help but wonder if she could touch the moon simply by reaching out her hand. She resisted the yelps from her throbbing arm and hand. Somehow her black cloth deflected most of the damage from the bullet of solid shadow, absorbing its darkness and leaving a white diamond outlined in crimson, reminiscent of the Day Star.

The horizon to the east warmed up; the morning was almost upon her. Hundreds of hoverships fled towards the west. Zulayka made her way to the peak of the obsidian pyramid. Its barren hallways lamented their abandonment. Zulayka was hopeful. If these capital officials felt the need to flee, then her Revolutionaries were doing well. Mayar managed to turn the tide.

Strangely, as Zulayka climbed upwards towards Bliss' office, the building's flesh seemed to tremble with a purr of an engine. The building's lights remained on. The power outage didn't seem to make it all the way up here.

Past one final hallway lined with portraits of former Leaders of Nardeban, an ornate door blocked her path. It was carved from black ashwood, with the history of Nardeban etched into its ancient body. Twelve panels now covered its face, each depicting a major event in Nardeban history. The first displayed the crashing of the ships, the moment that initiated humanity's New Age. The following panels portrayed the rise of Nardeban and the rebuilding of humanity on the new land, cut off from their home. She read these descriptions over and over again. They made no sense. These early panels were nothing like the history she had learned.

All the way down at the eleventh panel was the fall of the Insurgency. That should've been the end of it. The newly installed twelfth panel showed the first ships, but they weren't destroyed. A tendril of unease slipped through Zulayka. She opened the door and entered.

There he was, Leader Bliss. His pride rooted him to the spot, unwilling to run away like his compatriots. He looked at her with apathetic contempt. "Oh. You're here," he said lazily, pressing a button on his desk.

A thundering boom went off below them and Zulayka looked out the window to see the top of the pyramid split off from its base, soaring into the sky.

"Following the end of the Old Age, humanity lost the ability to space travel. Until today. Sort of. The murals must have surprised you." Bliss sounded tired, defeated.

"This thing can go to space? Carrying nearly all of Level 1?" Zulayka asked, scanning for any opportunity of escape. But there was none.

"It can. Or it was supposed to be able to. But it was never

finished, like that Autonomous Army. You were only battling the half-baked prototypes down there. Turns out vantablck engines aren't powerful enough to head into space. Eventually, this ship will burn up and crash back down to the earth, taking both of us down with it. I didn't waste any time like the Supervisor down there. Your fate was sealed the moment you entered this room. It's over, Zulayka. The Revolution ends here."

Zulayka laughed. "You missed a couple Revolutionaries down there. I already know what you're going to say, Bliss. And it's wrong."

Bliss shook his head, leaning back against a wall as they both tumbled higher and higher. "The Revolution won't stand a chance. I've instructed the rest of the remaining army to do their utmost to eliminate that whole Revolutionary council, leaving the Revolutionaries defenseless and leaderless. Maybe you've beaten me. But others like me will come and take over with time. It'll probably even be one of your own, someone who deviates and winds us right back on the path I set."

"You say that with a lot of confidence for a guy who tried to wipe the heads of a movement and only ended up wrangling himself into a full out war for the next one. Regardless of what happens from here on out, this is a victory. This is the start of something new. I have no doubt we'll continue to confront your kind, those who bend to the whispers of their soul. But how can we ever lose to you, when we're not playing the same game?"

Ignoring her, Bliss marched on, "People like you, people like Abraham, they're outliers. If I let you survive, you might've gone crooked at some point. It's human nature, Zulayka. That's why I will always win."

Zulayka strolled over to his desk, sitting down in his seat. "Neither Abraham nor myself were exceptional. You missed the point of all this, Bliss. Human nature is exactly what you should fear. The seed of light exists in everyone. It blooms for those who pull out the weeds, who secure its water, who breathe purity into it, who take it out of the shade and into the day.

"You might die here today, Bliss, but I won't."

Bliss laughed. "You're delusional. Insane."

Zulayka faced the falling sky. "You're the delusional one. I'm about to live forever." Her heart flew far, far from the earth. A creeping terror clogged Bliss' lungs and jogged through his veins, paralyzing him as death breathed over his neck.

***

Falaq raced towards the capital, with the sun squinting from the edge of the sky. After hours of flying, Pyra encompassed his vision. And up above it, he witnessed a blazing red pyramid hurtle back down to the ground. It was harshly beautiful. Scraps of metal shed from its side like flaming petals from a dying rose, with its smoke reaching the fading moon. At the top of the beheaded capital, a flag bearing the Day Star was raised high, billowing in the wind.

***

Falaq and Mayar sat with their knees bent underneath them. A light drill rested by Falaq's side, and Zulayka's gravestone sat in front of him, freshly planted next to the markers for Abraham and Isaac. The lone tree by Zahra's's grave towered above them, its leaves flaming in scarlet hues. Dozens of Mayar's engineered trees freckled the landscape, but here was the truest one, the tree whose roots sank the deepest and curled around the heart of the planet.

"We should return to the Lighthouse soon. The people need their Caretaker," Mayar said.

"We still have time, Mayar." Falaq went silent again. "Can you believe a year has passed?

"This loneliness remains with me every day. I used to imagine our ordeals would lighten after Nardeban. Instead, we're witnessing Bliss' warning, his curse," Falaq spoke somberly.

Mayar nodded. "So many things have changed. But despite what we've uncovered, you survived your first year as Caretaker, brother. Surely this is a sign."

Falaq closed his eyelids with the weight of worlds unknown. "Does that loneliness still bite into you, like storm clouds on the horizon?"

"It does," Mayar replied. "But the others ignore our warnings. They do not see the rain. I did not expect that darkness to persist."

"Not everyone can see the moon in broad daylight. You will always have me, Mayar."

"I know, brother."

The two basked under the shade of Isaac's tree. Their shadows melted in its cool embrace.

With the fall of Nardeban, the Revolutionaries founded the government of the Lighthouse. As Revolutionary council members were assassinated by the Remnants—the forces still loyal to Bliss—Falaq arose as a clear leader. He was declared the Caretaker by unanimous vote. His knowledge far surpassed the others, and his vision pierced further. Inaugurated by the death of Zulayka, one of his dearest mentors, Falaq placed Mayar by his side and the two were even more inseparable. They shared one breath.

In the aftermath, Caretaker Falaq abolished the levels, the levels that originated in his home of Kaam, the levels that separated without separating. Gone were the upper levelers and abysswalkers. He walked on, with Mayar by his side, forging reality through imagination.

With the emergence of the dawn came a broken peace. Unrest lingered among the former upper levelers, who glared in horror as the levels slowly came down. The revitalization of the earth brought the skyscrapers tumbling down. The world was slowly being deconstructed. Falaq was faced with the question of what to replace it with.

For the past year, Mayar strained at uncovering the secret behind Bliss' door and its twelve panels. The ruined spaceship, the plot where Zulayka's soul bloomed and Bliss' form wilted, held mysteries in its frayed wires and told stories through its strangely light metallic hull. To learn of Bliss' plans for the future, Mayar was forced to drill into the secrets of the past. The true origin of Nardeban still eluded him.
"Leave me be, Mayar. I'll meet you back at the hovercar."

Wordlessly, Mayar left his brother, his teacher.

***

Falaq sniffed. The air smelled of jasmine. His nose led him to a pellet of soil slightly darker than the rest. He wrestled a small jasmine flower free of the dirt. He breathed it in deeply, and his legs lifted themselves up. Without direction, without control, his feet marched forward. They rhythmically stepped for hours until they reached a collapsed steel tent in the middle of what used to be Midan's Level 5.

His hand leaped to the door, wrenching it open, and his heart eagerly, desperately, wonderfully looked inside.

Falaq fell onto his knees. His mind raced with Zulayka's story of Abraham and how the Insurgency was founded. How they learned the Tale of Ashura.

There, amid the wrecked walls and fractured floor, stood an aged woman. The fallen building cast too many shadows to view her clearly, only a tiny opening softly spilt a stream of light down upon her green hijab. The bottom of her ancient cane was stamped into the ground.

Falaq tried to speak, but the words slipped loose like the water from a pierced flask. He tried to use his arms to push himself off from the earth, but it was as if his arms were gone. All that flew were the tears pulsing across his face, slowly floating droplet by droplet into the light. A pain cracked and splintered across his chest, like shattering ice, as if his heart were shot by the arrow of sorrow.

"Your brother is a fine man. He is lucky to have one such as you as his teacher," she spoke. Each word pinned Falaq down, each word lifted Falaq up.

Falaq could only gaze in wonder, his flying tear drops sailing through the air like the golden dust revealed by the sun's ray.

"He will help you find the way back home. And you will

guide them all there." The scent of jasmine intensified.

With words she had only ever spoken to one before, she told Falaq, "Treasure your brother, and nurture him. As I treasured mine, and as he nurtured me."

She turned around. Her face burst forth from Falaq's memory, a memory of words and stories, a memory of truth. The staff carried her outside of the tent, and as she passed him all Falaq could see, all Falaq could hear was the scent of jasmine. The dream was tinted in tinges of green.

***

An acorn fell on Falaq's head, rousing him from his slumber. He remained sitting by the graves of his teacher, as if he had never moved. Holding the acorn in his palm, Falaq set off to plant it. A poem composed itself in his heart.

***

Water melts to flame, honey cools to iron
Tears float into light as I yearn
For a glimpse of your identity
You burnt today into eternity
You passed your torch, the torch was you
You were the wood, you were the fire, you were the smoke
O flaming rose I stare into your hues
Till I caught fire and awoke
Your reflection, my reflection
One direction, one perfection
I was the wood, I was the fire, I am the smoke
Rising, rising endlessly
To the spiralling clouds
Ode to Zulayka, the martyr from the falling sky, from the
collections of Falaq

This book was produced by
The Farthest Lote Tree Foundation

Visit us and view our other projects at *www.farthestlotetree.com*